INVISIBILIA

INVISIBILIA

STORIES

TOM HOWARD

SL/.NT
BOOKS

INVISIBILIA
Stories

First edition

Howard, Tom
    Invisibilia / by Tom Howard -- 1st ed.

ISBN 978-1-63982-221-8 (hardcover)
ISBN 978-1-63982-220-1 (paperback)
ISBN 978-1-63982-222-5 (ebook)

Library of Congress Control Number: 2026937020

Slant Books
P.O. Box 60295
Seattle, WA 98160

www.slantbooks.org

To my parents,

who encouraged me even when I came home from school with a prize, at the age of ten, for a story I wrote about a "funny cannibal detective."

I know that wasn't easy.

Contents

Heart of Gold | 1

Invisibilia | 22

Homecoming | 33

Metamorphosis | 44

Babel | 53

The Night Parade | 69

Disappearing Act | 87

Jellyfish | 98

Cary Grant at the Orpheum Theatre | 100

Swan Song | 117

The Long Shadows | 129

Acknowledgments | 151

Heart of Gold

WE'VE FALLEN IN LOVE. In lust. In something, anyway. In any case, we have fallen. We tumble madly, swooning for the Bellamys.

Even their name means *beautiful.*

It's been two weeks now since they moved in. David and Jasmine. They're in their twenties, early thirties at the latest. He's a throwback movie star, Paul Newman with broader shoulders, tall and tanned and almost preternaturally healthy-looking, as if he wakes up by rolling off a Ralph Lauren magazine ad. She's more old-school beauty. Mike says she looks like Cleopatra, and I can see that. Honey-colored, thin but shapely, with a yoga instructor's butt and Arctic-blue eyes. We live in a high-end part of suburban Washington, full of nice homes—our own is smaller but expensive—but the people here don't look like Paul Newman and Cleopatra. Even the Jennifers look bland and weathered by comparison.

"Her skin must be like butter," I say. "And I mean the really good butter, the exotic stuff."

"Sure," says Mike. He's standing by the island, reading the news on his phone and sipping coffee while I watch the Bellamys through the kitchen window. "The kind that's infused with orchid petals and whatnot."

Our houses face each other on the cul-de-sac. Out on the Bellamy driveway, Paul Newman leans down to kiss Cleopatra's neck as they stand, perfect torso to perfect torso, beside his Mercedes. The morning sunlight glints off her eyes, dazzling me. She doesn't lift her foot as he kisses her, but I feel as if she does. I feel like a better human being for having seen this.

"You don't understand." I turn to him. "When she smiles, a thousand angels get—"

"Wings?" he asks, still reading his phone.

"Erections."

Mike looks up, nods. "So gross."

"He kissed her *neck,*" I say, turning back to the window. "That's foreplay. That's essentially foreplay. Before *going off to work.*"

"Maybe her lips are dirty. Scabbed."

"*That's* gross. And blasphemy." I take our cups to the sink and rinse them, place them in the dishwasher. "I think I can see them glowing sometimes. Is that possible? Is it possible they're actually glowing?"

"No."

For two weeks I've watched them. In a friendly and completely non-skulking way. It's not that either of them is perfect. I haven't yet found any physical flaws, but I assume they're not perfect. Maybe he has thick, coarse back hair, or a porn addiction, or something. She may have a secret moustache. She may wake up at four in the morning every day to tend to her secret moustache. I'm nothing if not a realist. It's just that they just look so damn young. So untouched by anything. And more than that, they look as if they're genuinely in love. It's in the small things, the gestures: the neck kisses, the tilt of her head when she listens to him, the way he scoops up their daughter with such abandon when she runs out to greet him.

Their daughter. Oh dear God. Lacey. I thought it was Tracy at first—her mother never yells the name (obviously!), so it isn't easy picking it up when I'm out killing things in the garden or standing by an open window. Clearly not a Tracy! She's a china-doll version of her mother, the same light blue eyes, the same perfect face but dimpled with baby fat. She can't be older than four or five. By the tilt of her head and the way she watches the other neighborhood children from the shadows of the Bellamy porch, I can see she's shy, quiet, unusually thoughtful. I've spotted her on the porch with a book in hand. A book! Probing little being of light.

"Is today the big day?" Mike asks.

He means the day I make contact. I introduced myself to Jasmine the day they moved in, walking past with Ernest Hemingway Junior, our miniature dachshund. But I haven't yet gone over for a full-fledged conversation, the kind where she invites me in and we bond over petit fours and mimosas. Three times now I've been thwarted, by the weather and diabolical delivery people and not having any good reason to go over. "You think it's funny. But she's *basically* my best friend, only in the future, and we're both denied our friendship here in the past, or rather the present. It's like *grief.*"

"Hmm."

I wave a dish towel at him. "If you lost your best friend, wouldn't you grieve that you didn't get to spend more time together, doing friend things? So why not *also* grieve that you didn't spend more time together in the other direction, before you met?"

"Your logic," he says.

"Is?"

He arches an eyebrow. "Just that. I'm trying to identify what that was." He reaches an arm around my waist, leans down to place his mouth on my neck, tickling me with his stubble. The stubble is a new thing. He says it goes with the salt-and-pepper hair and the new wrinkles he's "growing" around his eyes. Grizzled chic, he calls it. It's an annoyingly good look for him.

"That doesn't feel awful," I admit, still looking out the window. David drives off, and Jasmine waits a few beats before turning her perfect butt in our direction, heads coolly back inside. My stomach flops.

"You taste good," he murmurs.

"Like butter?"

"Like butter made from angels."

Which makes me laugh.

My plan is to bring welcome brownies over sometime late in the morning, so I get started as soon as Mike leaves for work. I've never made brownies before but I find a recipe at DivineBrownieGoddess.com. DivineBrownieGoddess's real name is Rachel, and she says it's critical to use room-temperature eggs, so I remove the egg carton from the fridge and leave it on the counter. This feels like progress, like I'm delegating work to the eggs. I have no idea how long it takes for eggs to get to room temperature, but in my supervisory capacity I imagine it takes an hour, so I open my laptop and place it on the kitchen island and get busy.

For the last few years I've been doing freelance editing of women's erotica. Right now I'm editing *Moon of the Black Wolf*, a novel of forbidden werewolf love written by my friend Anna. We met at a writing workshop in the city. I was working on a novel about a woman who miscarries because she's secretly an alcoholic. It was also a detective story and a buddy comedy. Anna's story for the workshop was about a woman who one day tells her husband she can only get off if he dresses up for her. So he dresses up as Little Bo Peep, and then as Snow White, and then as the Little Match Girl, and she has mind-blowing orgasms. It turns out she's discovered he's having an affair and she's getting revenge by asking him to dress up, but by the end they love the outfits and the orgasms so much they decide to stick together. Anna and I hit it off right away. When I abandoned my own novel a while later and conceded, at Mike's urging, that I needed something to fill my time, I accepted Anna's offer to edit the book she was trying to sell. She ended up with a three-book deal, and passed my name around to her erotica buddies as her editor of choice. It keeps me busy.

The chapter I'm editing includes "the big knotting scene," according to Anna. I'm not familiar with the term so I have to look it up. In the writing group we talked a lot about verisimilitude. One writer in our group used to just say the word "verisimilitude" when he wanted to offer a criticism. He'd say it very seriously and with a good deal of self-satisfaction. Anna and I now say it all the time, for no reason, because we found it so entertaining.

For my abandoned novel, I attended AA meetings for two months so I could learn how alcoholics hid their drinking problems from spouses. One man said he'd pour vodka into water bottles and keep them in his office. He always kept the vodka in Dasani water bottles, he said, so he wouldn't get them confused with the other bottles. Aquafina was for white rum. Poland Spring was just Poland Spring. I started drinking during the day just to see what it was like. It was a mild, short-term alcoholism, for purposes of verisimilitude.

The knotting scene should gross me out more than it does. I make a few notes about the characters' physical positioning in the scene, the improbability of the angles of insertion and so on, then trim the dialogue down. Anna gives me carte blanche on the dialogue. Overall it's a solid chapter, though. Disgusting but solid.

I take a break to bond with Ernie. He's eight now, and we should be closer. I think he mistrusts me because I once drove home from the dog park without him. I remembered quickly enough, but when I drove back I found him apart from the other dogs, eyeing the parking lot in a way that would have to be considered woeful. Mike had Ernie Senior when we first met, and when he passed on—that's how we talked about it, as if the dog had advanced to a higher level of being—Mike thought getting a dog of my very own would be therapeutic. That was a year after the miscarriage. I think sometimes that Ernie knows he's a double replacement dog. For Ernie Senior and for the baby I lost. Hard to live up to that, I imagine.

Ernie lets me rub his stomach as our bonding activity. After ten minutes of this, I remember the eggs, the brownies, and Jasmine Bellamy. Once the brownies are in the oven, I set the timer, go up to shower, then take my time straightening my hair and finding the right outfit, as well as a good angle in the mirror. Standing halfway behind the door seems best. I need something casual, but intelligent, but sexy, but effortless, but striking, but unremarkable. Something effortlessly glorious. Then I realize nothing in my closet will look anything but casual to Jasmine, which makes it easier.

An hour later I'm at her door, heart-shaped brownie plate in one hand and a bottle of Veuve Cliquot in the other. After ringing the bell I turn to look out at the cul-de-sac. Our house is the oldest of the six on the street, and the smallest, though still in my mind absurdly large. The place Mike and I had in Petworth, in the city, was fifteen hundred square feet, and you couldn't open the refrigerator door if someone was standing behind you. But it was in the city. I could walk to the coffee shop. I could walk to the metro. I could, if I wanted, walk by the old Lincoln Cottage six blocks away. In my abandoned novel, my heroine is visited by the ghost of Mary Todd Lincoln, who—this is true—once sewed fifty-six thousand dollars of government bonds inside her petticoats, before her oldest and only surviving son had her committed to an asylum. I thought that would make my heroine seem quirky.

Inside the Bellamy house I hear noises, voices, but no one comes to the door. I ring the bell a second time. Through the sidelight I have a narrow, clouded view of the great room. I know it's the great room because I dragged Mike into the house one night when it was under construction. I think I see Lacey sitting on the floor in the middle of the room. The muffled sound I'm hearing could be her cries.

I should just leave. In thirty seconds I'll leave.

Somewhere behind me a front door slams. Without turning I know it's the blond-headed twin sons of one of the Jennifers, tearing out of the house at the end of the cul-de-sac. They start bouncing a basketball as loudly as I imagine it's possible to bounce a basketball, and immediately their voices are joined by others, all boys. It sounds like a hail of rubber bullets, the summer afternoon coming under siege.

Jasmine slips into view behind the glass, dressed in yoga pants and a sleeveless top. She squats down, with her back to the door, to face her daughter. Talks to her in what I imagine is a soothing, honey-soaked voice. I'm admiring her back muscles—marveling that there are such things as back muscles—when I watch her grip the little girl by the shoulders and shake her, twice, hard.

I turn quickly and leave, embarrassed by what I've seen.

At two o'clock Mike calls. He calls every day at two o'clock. I set aside Anna's manuscript on the laptop and tell him what happened.

"So we have brownies at home," is all he says.

"I threw them out. You're funny."

"Nobody knows anything," he says.

It's one of his lines, a Mike-ism. He says it to remind me not to read too much into anything. Because we can Never Really Know what's going on in someone else's life, in someone else's head. Which I get. Obviously. Be generous with people, Mike says.

"I'm not saying anything," I tell him. "I obviously don't have experience raising children."

"And yet," he says, with terrible patience.

"It's just that obviously she has problems. The girl."

"Interesting," Mike says.

"I mean yes, of course my initial thought was different. But then. Then I thought—you'd be proud of me—I thought, I shouldn't just *assume* anything."

"I'm always proud of you."

"Sure. Anyway I thought, what if the little girl just has all these problems we don't know about? As perfect as she looks? I mean, maybe she's one of those kids who slams her head against the wall when you're not looking."

"That's a thing?"

"Maybe. I believe it is." I drum my fingers on the counter. "I mean I'm not sure, even if that were true, that you'd necessarily *shake* a kid as a solution."

"Maybe her shoulders were out of alignment," Mike suggests.

"You're not even trying." I sigh. "Home early?"

"Ish. Feed Ernie. Be good."

At six-thirty Mike calls to say he's running late and for me to eat without him. The thought of eating leftover vegetarian lasagna alone at the island saddens me, so I make myself two pieces of toast and pour a vodka tonic and stand by the kitchen window, looking out over the cul-de-sac. The Two Jennifers are on the sidewalk in front of the Bellamy house, talking with Jasmine. I should capitalize on the opportunity and go out to join them, introduce myself, but I don't. For one thing, I can't bring the brownies and champagne out with the Two Jennifers standing by—it would look as if I were trying to show them up. For another thing, they always look right through me. Or not through me exactly, but just over my shoulder, as if they're keeping an eye on someone or something far more interesting fifty feet behind me and to the left. It's an odd phenomenon that began a few months after the miscarriage. First they took pity on me, and then, when they discovered I had no interest in getting pregnant again, they simply moved on. Or maybe I was left behind. When I was around them I felt as if I were dead, as if my ghost were only flickering at the edge of their vision.

For my writing group I wrote a short story called "Dead Woman," about a woman named Marie who haunts various houses in her neighborhood. She stands in hallways and watches her neighbors sleep, looks over their belongings, has some encounters with family pets, touches things to mark her presence. Moves things around just a little. *I was here*, she thinks. *I was alive here, once.* The twist is she's not actually a ghost. She thinks she is, but really she has a neurological disorder called Cotard's syndrome. I'd read a story about a soldier in England who had it. He slowly starved himself because he thought he was already dead, and therefore had no reason to eat. So I afflicted Marie with Cotard's syndrome. She'd also had a miscarriage, but it wasn't relevant to the story. I had her crawl in one house through a doggy door in the back, an idea I found in an online forum for reformed burglars to share security tips. I tested the idea out on a house down the street when the family was away on vacation, just to make sure it would really work. In the story that's when you realize something's going on with Marie, when she's shimmying through the doggy door in her pajamas. That's when you're like: what the fuck, Marie. Then the family who lives in the house wakes up and finds her hovering in the kitchen. The kids start screaming. Marie thinks they're afraid of her because she's a ghost. That's the funny part of the story. The writing group said I needed more humor. *Fear me not*, she wails, *fear me not, my children*. Waving her arms spookily / comically. The police arrive and Marie slips away and sneaks out the back door. But the police have the place surrounded, and when she comes outside they shine a massive spotlight on her. She still thinks she's a ghost so she ignores them when they tell her to freeze, and keeps walking toward the light. So they shoot her and kill her. ("The story ends a little abruptly" was the common thread in the criticism from the writing group.)

Outside, one of the Jennifers points to each of the houses on the cul-de-sac in turn, while Jasmine listens, smiles, nods, says nothing. When the Jennifer's arm swings around and points in the direction of our house, I slink back from the window and carry my drink and my toast to the other room.

Later Mike and I lie together on the sofa and I let him rub my feet while we watch "Home Dream Home." Mike likes the show because he says it gives him ideas for our retirement. I like the show because the couples always have amusing and inexplicable jobs. Tonight, a couple from Portland, Oregon is looking for a home on Bali. The husband from Portland designs grandfather clocks. His wife runs a meditation center for troubled cats. They're looking to spend no more than two and a half million.

I ask him if he's heard from Tina lately. Immediately I regret it, and I apologize.

"Where'd that come from?" he asks in the space that follows. He stops rubbing my feet but keeps his hands on me. This isn't a fight, is what he's saying.

"The cat thing," I say. Tina had a cat, or perhaps still has one. That's how I found out. Mike kept coming home covered in cat hairs. It was two years after the miscarriage. They never fucked, he said. It was just an emotional affair, an emotional affair that included him being around her cat. I think, looking back, he wanted to be caught. Not to get out of the marriage, but to make something change. I told him that made sense. I knew it hadn't been easy. *I* hadn't been easy. He said he loved me and wanted to make it work, and he hated the thought that he'd broken my heart. You didn't, I said, and somehow that was true, though it was terrible to say. Not long after, I began writing a story about a married woman named Etta who gives a blowjob to a stranger outside a bar. She doesn't know why. Then she goes home and has great sex with her husband. The sex is explicitly rendered. I mean, I didn't just say "she had great sex with her husband." The word *cock* gets thrown around a lot. Etta decides she likes it, the thrill of the secret blowjob and how she feels afterward and the incredible marital sex. She doesn't really know why. I figured I'd discover the reason as I wrote the story, or that in the end it wouldn't matter. My plan was for her to start placing personal ads to find men during the day. I hadn't gone down on Mike in quite a while at that point—it just seemed to fall off the regular rotation after the miscarriage and everything—so to research the story, I created an online ad saying I was a married woman looking to give oral pleasure. I just wanted to see what the responses would be like, how men would describe themselves and try to stand out. I began corresponding with a man named Frank, or at least he told me his name was Frank. I told him my name was Clementine. Frank said he had an average-sized penis, was in a sexless marriage, and did Renaissance fair reenactments every other weekend in the summer, which I found charmingly stupid. I wanted to understand the logistics of how it might work, so we planned a meeting. He suggested we meet at a park, a park they used for reenactments, during one of the off-weeks. He said maybe I could go down on him in his car while he kept lookout. I agreed. I wasn't planning to go. But then I decided it was important to know what my character would be thinking as she drove to give this person a blowjob, if she would be nervous, or excited, or guilt-ridden, or all or none of those things. But I also knew I wasn't going to do anything, so it was hard to know if I had verisimilitude there. I decided I'd get in the car with Frank, which was risky, but also the only true way to inhabit my character. Once I was in the car (I imagined all this, on my way to the park) I'd tell him I was really a writer, and apologize, and that would be that. There was the possibility I might have to put him in my mouth for a few seconds as a show of good faith. I decided that would be fine as long as it went absolutely no further. I pulled into the park and waited for an hour, but Frank never showed up. I never ended up writing that story. I was going to call it "The Head Mistress."

On television, the grandfather clock designer and the cat therapist are discussing if they can make it work even though the master bedroom's walk-in closet is inadequate.

"You know I love you," Mike says. Rubbing my feet again.

I close my eyes. "I know it," I tell him. And the thing is, it's true. I do know it. I really do.

Later in the week I have lunch with Anna and we talk through *Moon of the Black Wolf.* I tell her I'm starting to like the werewolf but I can't figure out yet if I'm supposed to like the heroine.

"Do you have to like her?" she asks.

We're sitting at an outside table at a restaurant near the old house at Petworth, drinking mimosas. Anna is younger than me, with good skin and wonderful fake boobs, but she also has hard lines around her mouth and eyes, which she calls divorce lines. She says she could pay to remove them but she doesn't. Her eyes look bright and young, though. They look merry. Right now they're hidden behind dark sunglasses which reflect my own dark sunglasses back at me.

I shrug. "You know your audience."

"I know nothing," she says.

The server comes past and I tip the champagne glass, say I'll have a second. Anna lowers her sunglasses as the server walks away, notes, "I think that's three. I add because I care."

I move lettuce from one side of the salad bowl to the other, then go to work separating the walnuts and the bean sprouts. "I've been baking lately," I tell her. "Well not really. But I might start."

"That's fascinating. So, hey. Dawn wanted me to ask you again. About the thing."

Dawn's her editor. Her real editor, I mean, at the publishing house. The thing is a part-time job.

"Ask me again in a year," I say. "Five years. Tell Dawn to keep the seat warm for me for five years."

"Just think it might be good."

"Might be, sure." I accept the drink from the server, then lean forward to say, "My plate is full right now, is the thing. My salad bowl is full."

"I see that." Anna sits back and appraises me silently, draws conclusions, fills gaps in the negative space between us, and then moves on in a span of a few seconds. "Well. How do I get you to like my heroine then?"

"Show me," I say, "that she's got a good heart."

CLOUDS ARE ROLLING in by the time I get to my car in the parking lot, and it's raining as I leave the city. I pull into the cul-de-sac and as I do, I see Lacey Bellamy standing on the corner in the rain, soundlessly crying.

After parking the car, I grab an umbrella and retrieve the girl. She takes my hand and lets me walk her to the covered porch. Leaning down and pulling my head close to hers so she can hear me above the rain, I ask her where her mother is. She tells me she doesn't know, gathering panicked lungfuls of breath between each syllable. I place my hand on the doorknob and twist. The door swings open.

"Let's go inside and wait for her to come back," I say.

The house is predictably gorgeous. Dark hardwood floors, cavernous stone fireplace, Sub-Zero and Wolf in a kitchen of glittering steel. I follow Lacey to the living room and we sit amidst her books and toys. I ask her questions to distract her but she refuses to answer, only sets about the task of arranging a sort of domestic diorama on the floor, Barbie in a glittering black-and-gold gown rocking a baby panda to sleep in its crib.

There's a thumping above us. Lacey and I both stop and look toward the ceiling. Seconds later, Jasmine comes down. She's dressed in sweats and a tank top. Her hair is pulled back and her face is red and puffy, as if she's been crying. Or sleeping.

"Oh my god," she says.

Rising to my feet, I say, "She couldn't find you, that's all."

"Bad," Lacey says, her body tense, her small voice almost a whisper.

"I'm Kay. From across the street. Welcome to the neighborhood." I'm aware of how ridiculous this sounds. "Look, I should go." Behind me, I hear Lacey's feet pad across the rug back to the sofa.

"I'm sorry," Jasmine says, though I'm not sure if she's speaking to me or to her daughter. She leans back for a moment against the wall, and I can see her mentally drawing a breath. Even in her sweats, even sleep-addled—or is it something else?—she's stunning. "Fuck," she adds. "Having a day, you know. You ever have one of those?"

I nod. "Couple years' worth."

That brings a wary smile. Up close, I can see she's younger than I thought. The makeup—and her height, and her figure, and her attractiveness—hides her youth.

"I'm not doing anything right now," I say. "If you need a break, I mean." Which I realize must sound offensive, coming from someone she doesn't know.

Jasmine starts to say something, which I'm guessing will be *What the hell does that mean?* But she stops herself, and looks down at the floor, and then puts her hands on her head and looks back at me. Studies me, or herself. "Okay," she says.

"Show me what you got," I say to Lacey.

We're upstairs in Lacey's bedroom while Jasmine sleeps on the sofa. After a half-hour of reading aloud—she reads better than most of the adults in my old writing group—Lacey is now giving me a comprehensive tour of her dollhouse, a two-story Arts and Crafts number with a wraparound porch and gazebo in the back. It's the size of my first apartment out of college. We lie on the floor beside the dollhouse and discuss what they're doing inside, and Lacey suggests that maybe *they're* lying on the floor together too, the doll house people, looking into an even smaller dollhouse.

"And inside *that* dollhouse?" I ask.

"Even smaller one," she says quietly, eyes wide. Then she freezes as a thought strikes her, and she sits up straight and looks toward her bedroom window.

"Worth checking," I say. We both stand and go to the window, but we see no giant eyeballs looking in on us.

"Yeah, worth checking," she says. Ruefully, I think. She takes my hand and leads me back down to the floor.

I ask if she has a secret name.

"What's a secret name?"

"A name," I say, "that you wish you had but you don't. I had one as a little girl."

Her eyes are saucers of aquamarine. "Can you tell me?"

"Technically no. I mean, it's a secret, right? But I'm old now so I can tell you. It was Clementine."

She laughs. It's a light, airy sound, like bells ringing in some farther room.

"It's true. My dad used to sing this song about a girl named Clementine, and I thought it sounded pretty. It's what I told my dolls to call me."

"And did they?" she asks.

I nod. "Otherwise, you know—I had to pop their heads off." Which makes her laugh again, and her laughter makes me laugh.

Jasmine opens the door some time later. She walks me downstairs to the door, gives me a quick hug. She smells like vanilla and honeysuckle.

"Thank Miss Kay," she tells her daughter.

"Just Kay."

Lacey waves me down, so I crouch low until we're face-to-face. She cups her delicate hand to her mouth and whispers in my ear. "Charlotte," she says. "My secret name is Charlotte."

THE NEXT DAY, Jasmine waves to me from the porch as I'm finishing a walk with Ernie. Lacey, seeing the dog, runs down the steps to greet him.

"She keeps asking for one," Jasmine says, a little later. We're sitting on the porch while Lacey rolls on the grass with the dog.

"I'll ask Ernie if he's available."

There's no trace of the Jasmine I saw yesterday. Gone is the helplessness, the sense of disorder about her. Her hair, her face, her summer clothes—everything is put together. She looks *at ease.* Not only with her body but with everything. Seeing her on the porch, her long legs catching the sunlight, I'm struck by how well she fits here. I'd thought she didn't belong in this neighborhood, just as I don't belong, but I see now that I was wrong.

"I want to apologize," she says, dropping her voice so Lacey won't overhear. "Just about yesterday. About the way I was. And you—you were great."

I shrug this off. "The kid's easy. And sweet."

"Easy," she says, and I can't tell if she's agreeing with me or not. Then: "Guess I'll be the talk of the town now." She tilts her head at me for a moment, then looks away. "Sorry. Just seems like the kind of neighborhood where things get around."

"You mean the Jennifers." When she looks a question at me, I say: "The blondes."

She smiles at this. "Oh. I thought one of them was named, like, Janelle?"

"But which one?" I ask. "I can never remember."

She laughs, and it's the same bell-like laugh of her daughter's. "I think I like you," she says, leaning back again in the chair.

"Then it's all going according to plan."

Now Lacey is leading Ernie, or being led by Ernie, in a high-speed chase around and around the cherry tree in the center of the front yard.

"She really is a great kid," says Jasmine. "She just gets anxious sometimes. Wandering outside in the rain—that's new. My fault. I should've. . . . I don't know why it's hard sometimes."

"Everyone gets tired," I say.

"Not everyone hides in the guest room to take a nap."

I'm not sure what the response to this might be, so I let it sit there between us.

"Can I tell you something?" Her voice, now, is even lower. She's still cool, still in control, but she isn't looking at me. "I didn't want a baby," she says. "I was twenty. Jesus."

I nod, though she isn't looking my way. "Tough situation."

She shakes her head. "It's *selfish*. But then, then. You know how you're supposed to just fall for the kid when she's born? I just—didn't. I love her, you know. I swear I do. But I didn't feel that thing you're supposed to feel." She looks me, finally, in the eye. "How bad is that? To say that."

"Why did you tell me?"

She hesitates, chews her bottom lip. "Because you don't have kids. I know that sounds awful."

"Couldn't have kids," I say. "I have an incompetent cervix. So I'm told."

"Oh." She blinks. "Oh, I didn't mean—it's only that I heard. Well."

"Sure."

I never told them, the Jennifers, that I couldn't have children. I told them I didn't want any. That I was relieved after the miscarriage. I don't know why. To upset them, maybe. To distance myself from them. Their pity bothered me. And anyway, couldn't it be two things? Couldn't I be barren, or hopelessly damaged, and also have no interest in having children?

I suggest a babysitter. They can obviously afford one.

"David's against it. He says that wasn't the deal. First five years are critical. Formative." She pulls her legs up under her on the chair, and just like that she looks like a teenager. "Besides, she's great. You said it. *Easy.* I just get tired."

In the yard, Lacey is flat on her back, exhausted. The dog licks her face, making her laugh.

In the evening, Mike sits doing work on his laptop while I stretch out on the sofa and drink and watch "Home Dream Home." (He's a puppeteer. She designs leotards for little people. Their budget is a cool three million.) I tell him I talked with Jasmine. He doesn't know about yesterday's babysitting adventure.

"And?" he asks. "Was it everything you'd hoped?"

He's joking, but there's something less than charitable in his voice tonight, a sneaky indifferent cruelty that I'm probably only imagining. Maybe he's tired.

"She's just young," I say. "Younger than I thought. A sweet kid."

"Should invite them for dinner," he says.

"I should," I say. I sip my wine, and play with my loose tooth. It's on the left side, on the bottom. I should see someone about it but I haven't yet. I mean I can't imagine it's a good thing to have a loose tooth at my age. I can't imagine the dentist saying there's nothing to worry about there. Later, before the bathroom mirror, I try out my smile to see how it would look without the tooth. I decide I'll have to alter my smile. Nothing drastic. A forty-five watt smile. Mike may notice, or he may not. He may just think it's a sign of my advancing age, like sagging breasts or far-sightedness. A winding-down of my smile.

As I fall asleep I think about the things Jasmine told me on the porch. I picture the four of us standing by the kitchen island, hanging out, cocktails in hand, while Lacey rolls on the floor with Ernie. I imagine David laying his hand on her shoulder, squeezing it, while he tells some story about their trip last year to Venice. Mike, touching my hair as he goes past to check the oven, letting his fingers slide across my waist as he tells his own story about the time we got lost in Florence in the rain, leaving out everything in the story that mattered. Both men, laying claim.

~

Later, in bed, we have great sex. I think it's great sex. In any case I'm very vocal. To turn myself on I try to imagine Anna's sexy werewolf, but instead I keep picturing Marie, from my story, running out the back door into a spray of police gunfire. I say *Oh God* a lot.

"Okay," Mike says, in the dark, when it's over. "That was interesting."

"Interesting good?" I ask. Then I realize if I have to ask, it's probably not good. "Sorry. Tired I guess."

"Just talk to me," he says.

"Oh, Mike." I turn toward him, though we're both invisible to each other. "Haven't we talked everything out?" I try to say it tenderly.

He says, "We can't change things by wishing for them, love."

I put my hand on his cheek, rough and warm. "Can't we?" I ask.

"Ah, babe." He sighs and rolls over.

Once, I wished to not be pregnant, and then I wasn't any more. The doctors said it might have been, probably was, congenital—my incompetent cervix. Mike believed that. I didn't tell him the truth, that I'd made it happen, until much later. This was after Tina. I told him I was sorry. My magic was weak, I told him. Like my cervix. That's why, though I'd only wished for this one thing to die, everything else was poisoned too.

~

The place we had in Petworth was small, but it had a private garden in the back, with a stone bench in which two gargoyles had been carved on either side. I could never grow anything—it was all just wildflowers and weeds after the first season we moved in—but I liked sitting out there on the gargoyle bench, reading. An overgrown hedgerow shielded the garden from the neighbors. Because you stepped down into the garden, and it was hidden as it was, Mike called it my hollow. Kay's Hollow.

We sold the place to a younger couple who already had a child of their own. The Bradfords. They tore out the hedgerow as soon as they moved in, and made a proper vegetable garden. They got rid of the stone bench, too. After a few years they had another child, too. And they got a dog. Now they have a perfect little family of four, plus the dog, and they're still living there, which is how I know the house was always big enough for us.

At least once a week I drive by to see if it looks any different. Newspapers are piled on the front step this week. They vacation at Cape Cod for two weeks at the end of every summer. One of our old neighbors told me.

I pretend, sometimes, that they are us, or we are them.

As August moves on, I see Jasmine more. We don't become best friends. We don't drink mimosas and eat petit fours. But we talk. She talks, mostly, and I listen. She's lovely and effortlessly sensual and pleasingly honest, and I find myself rapidly losing interest. She asks me to help sometimes with Lacey, and I'm happy to oblige.

I make my way through Anna's novel. Turns out the werewolf isn't a werewolf. He's not a man who occasionally becomes a wolf but a wolf who occasionally becomes—terribly—a man, and when he lies dying at the end, he's revealed in his lovely, natural lupine form. When I get to the end, I cry for twenty minutes. Then I pour myself a drink.

Two o'clock passes, and the phone doesn't ring.

"What do you miss the most?" I asked Mike, once.

We were sitting on the deck of a house we'd rented at Lake Anna, early evening on the last day of a good trip we took last fall.

"About what?" he asked.

"Who we were."

Maybe it was the light going down. The way the shadows of the tall trees around the lake fell across us both. He looked old to me then, in that moment. That's why I asked him the question. I loved him still. But in his face I thought I saw all the ghosts of the men he'd once been, and I wondered.

His eyes tracked me through the shadows as if he could read my thoughts.

"I'll tell you," he said, and if he had a smile on his face, I couldn't see it. "We used to be," he said, "our favorite subject."

I don't know why I remember that now. But it's what comes to mind in the silence of the two o'clock phone call that doesn't come. The phone calls were Mike's idea, or the therapist's idea, I don't remember now. To rebuild trust. I said I didn't need them, didn't want them, and anyway he'd get tired of it eventually.

I open my laptop and take notes for a story. In the story, a woman's teeth are all falling out. One by one. She's a mother, with many children. She hides the truth from her husband, who is amazing, because with each tooth she loses, the lives of their children get better. Bonnie makes first violin chair, Duke loses his stutter, Elizabeth's rosacea clears up. Etc. Meanwhile she has this sandwich bag full of teeth she's hiding. She goes to the doctor and he says it won't end there. He means it won't end with the teeth. He shows her a picture of what she'll become, and the picture is of an old hag. Thin, brittle hair, a mole on her chin, a long hair growing out of the mole on her chin, a stooped back. The works. So she says to the doctor, Fix me, and he says, It'll cost you. Like, for each tooth he replaces, or any time he gives her back something she's lost, something bad has to happen to her husband or to one of the kids. She thinks about it for a long time. Then she says, Well, how bad exactly? That's the kicker. That's when you're like, Fuuuuuuuck.

I don't know what any of it means, or if it has to mean anything. I don't know how she feels about her children, or why her teeth are falling out in the first place, or why her amazing husband doesn't notice. Who wouldn't notice his wife turning into a hag?

I close the file without saving it, and then I call Anna.

"What is it?" she asks. "What's the matter?"

"Nothing," I say. "I finished your book."

"Okay, you sound weird. Why do you sound weird?"

I feel some sob building up in me that won't ever, can't ever be released. It's not even a sob. It might be laughter. I can't tell. "I get like this," I tell her, "at the end of things."

August winds down. The summer is dying away. It feels like it will be the last one, though I know it won't be. I think that every summer.

Maybe it's only that this morning felt different from other mornings. It's the little things. The quotidian details, as we used to say in the writing group. The new lines suddenly visible around the lines around my eyes in the mirror. The way my hand shook when I poured a vodka and orange juice. The fact that Mike's hand didn't linger on my shoulder before he left for work.

I'm writing up my final notes on Anna's manuscript but having trouble concentrating. Because of this being the end of everything. I set my notes aside, sip from the Aquafina bottle, and watch the shadows creep down the kitchen wall as the sun rises in the sky.

In my novel, the one I didn't finish, the heroine's name is Kate. Kate is riddled with guilt because of the miscarriage. She loves her husband but she keeps the truth from him, the truth that she killed their child. Then most of the novel is about Kate having these different adventures, surrounded by quirky characters. You sort of forget about the miscarriage and the alcoholism and all that. It's just fun, and you like Kate. She's endearing. You think she's on a quest, and you want her to be happy. But really she's about to hit rock bottom. That was my plan, at least. The novel faded away. I didn't get very far. But I had this big final scene in mind. I was going to have her survive all her adventures and then come home to her husband, and tell him some ridiculous lie to explain where she's been the whole book. And miraculously, stupidly, he believes her. Or maybe he doesn't believe her, but he accepts what she tells him. She can see that all he cares about is that she's home. Because he loves her, see. And you think: everything will be okay. Her secrets are safe. It's undeserved, it's completely undeserved, but as the reader you don't care—I want you not to care—because you want it to work out. Oh, how you want it to work out. Kate's husband goes off to work. She sits alone on the sofa for a while—I was going to really drag this part out, to up the tension—and then she all of a sudden gets up. Starts drinking. Drinks all day, just sitting there in the living room. She leaves the empty bottles of vodka and white rum on the coffee table. She hauls out her secret Dasani water bottles and drains them, throws them on the floor. Then she calls her husband and tells him to come home. She starts to black out and she thinks: This must be the end. I was going to end it with the sound of the garage door opening.

My phone buzzes. *I need you.* From Jasmine.

I sit for a while, listening to my breathing. It doesn't sound like mine. It sounds like an old woman's breathing. I force myself to breathe like myself again, easily, capriciously. Then I walk across the street, and put my arms around Jasmine, and tell her everything will be fine, and send her off to bed. When the door closes, I join Lacey in her room. We talk about the Little Prince and whether Ernie can see rainbows and what clouds might taste like. I ask if she wants to do errands with me, and she says yes.

We stop at the bank, then the dry cleaners. We grab frozen yogurt in Clarendon, and then stop for lunch—Mediterranean salads with French fries. It's warm outside but not humid. Clouds glide across the azure sky. I wonder if it'll be the last perfect day of the summer—because there will be a last perfect day, there always is, though we never know it until it's gone.

After lunch we drive to the grocery store, and I tell Lacey she can pick out anything she likes, her favorite things. When we're back in the car, I ask if she wants to play a game, and she nods eagerly.

"For this game," I say, "you will be Charlotte. And who will I be?"

She doesn't hesitate. "Clementine," she says, beaming.

"Bright girl."

It takes fifteen minutes to get to the old house. She talks nonstop, and though I'm listening to her and responding, I'm listening, too, for something else. For some signal. From what or whom I couldn't say. But I only feel lighter and lighter as the streets grow more familiar. There is no signal. By the time I find a parking spot around the corner from the house, I feel weightless. Like a girl myself.

I lead her around back, carrying the grocery bags. Through the gated fence and past the garden to a patio of dry-laid stone. The doggy door is too small for me now, but not for a four-year-old girl. She crawls through, grunting and giggling, as I watch for neighbors. Her feet slip through and then a second later the door swings open.

We explore together. Though I lived here once, it feels new again, and not only because the walls have been painted and the furniture replaced. Charlotte takes my hand. We talk in whispers at first, as we try out the sofa and the two small chairs in the living room, and look over the books on the shelves, and run our hands along the smooth granite counter in the galley kitchen, and delight in the miniature scalloped soaps and the mermaid-themed hand towels in the second bath. But her favorite room is the small second bedroom where the two Bradford girls sleep. It's less than half the size of her room at the Bellamy house, but hand-painted vines climb the pale lavender walls and ceiling, and rose petals float lazily on an imaginary breeze. She lies on one of the beds and sighs. "I wish," she says, "we could stay here."

We open all the windows in the house. Sounds as familiar as an old sweatshirt are carried into the house on the afternoon breeze—distant car horns, screen doors closing, music from a passing car, a far-off siren. Charlotte joins me in the kitchen to help with the brownies. I hold the eggs in my hands and wonder if they're warm enough. They are, I think. They must be. We slide the brownies in the oven and wait. While we wait, she tells me her secrets, and I tell her mine. Not all, though. Not all.

Here's a secret I don't tell. A few months ago I came out of the bedroom and overheard Mike on the phone with his sister, Jen. I knew it was Jen because Mike wasn't saying much, but now and then I heard him say, *Yeah, I think you made your point.* The first time I ever talked with Jen, when I came to Mike's parents' house for Thanksgiving a few months after we started dating, she pulled me aside to tell me how rough a time it had been for Mike. His ex had left him for a CrossFit trainer and was married and pregnant within a year. *The point is you can't break my little brother's fucking heart.* She'd been drinking a lot when we had this talk.

From the top of the staircase I heard Mike's half of the conversation:

Maybe, I don't know.

I never said that.

That's enough.

And then, after a seriously long pause:

Because she's got a good heart.

I walked away after that. I thought of asking him about it, but I didn't. It couldn't be something I wanted to hear. To have a good heart is to be secretly good, to be redeemable in some way invisible to the eye or the mind. And *because!* That's what killed me. That's an answer to another question, one I didn't, then, wish to know.

The afternoon slips quietly away. I remember Ernie, who hasn't been fed, and I turn my phone on briefly. Dozens of messages come through.

Without reading any of them, I turn the phone off and set it aside, and watch Charlotte as she sleeps beneath an afghan on the sofa. The light's starting to fall. I settle into the chair beside her and close my eyes. I'm tired.

I think: something, now, will happen.

A sharp sound wakes me. A car backfiring. I check the time and see it's grown late. The lights in the house are all off, but in the twilight I'm able to make my way to the sideboard and find candles and matches. I light two candles and bring them with me back to the living room, where Charlotte is stirring. She sits up in the flickering darkness and begins to cry.

"We're still playing the game," I tell her. "Just a little longer, Charlotte. First we'll have dinner."

I think: He'll come. He must come.

If he comes, it's because he understands everything. How can he not understand?

Sirens wail in the distance, then come closer, and closer still. My body tenses, then eases as the sound changes pitch and begins to fade.

"I'm afraid," whispers Charlotte.

I take her hand. "So am I," I tell her. "But it won't be long."

In her small hand I think I can feel her pulse, racing wildly. But it's my own heart I feel. I can almost hear it beat, trace its restless movement, an animal thrashing in its cage.

A car approaches. I let out a deep breath, not knowing I've been holding it in all this time, as the car's headlamps sweep across the walls of the dark room, and fill them with light.

Invisibilia

FOR A WEEK NOW we've been disappearing.

At first we thought it was only our mother, who we found in the kitchen one morning, partially translucent, eating a low-calorie muffin after coming back from Pilates class. Vi pointed and we watched silently, from behind, as a blob of muffin worked its way down her esophagus. This was followed by a swallow of black coffee, which went down faster. We couldn't watch either the muffin or the coffee go all the way down because the view was blocked by our mother's blue sleeveless workout top, which—like the muffin and the coffee, but unlike our mother—remained solid.

Hey, Vi said, you're see-through.

I'd been trying for a few seconds to come up with something to say, to figure out how to broach the subject. Vi's the direct one, the broacher. She says life is too short not to be. I tell her it's not *that* short, and she'll remind me of our cousin Ainsley, who died as an infant, when she was three days old. She hadn't even been given the name Ainsley yet. She was just The Baby. Aunt Liz and Uncle Matt only gave her a name so they'd have something to put on the death certificate. Vi will say sometimes: Ainsley never even knew her own name, and I can't live that way. Something about this doesn't make sense to me but I can never think of a good answer, one that won't make me sound like I'm indifferent to Ainsley's plight, so I mumble and change the subject.

Our mother turned. She looked like herself, mostly, except for the fact that parts of the kitchen were now faintly visible through her head, her arms, and her legs. She glanced down at her right hand; splayed the fingers so she could inspect them; rotated her wrist back and forth.

I feel okay, she said, blinking at us. I feel lighter.

Where's Dad? I asked. Does he know?

In the shed, she said. And yes, probably. He must. Right?

Are you solid? Vi asked.

I am to me, she said. Feel me.

We went to her and each took one of her hands. She never used to let us hold her hands, because she said holding hands made her too hot. Aunt Liz told us that our mother refused to hold hands with anyone even as a little girl, and once screamed at a crossing guard for trying to take her hand without permission. We jumped at the chance to do it now.

Soft but mostly solid, Vi announced. And sort of cold. Like a jellyfish.

Like holding a balloon filled with cool air, I said. Then I added, But in a nice way. Because I was worried she'd think I didn't like balloons filled with cool air, and maybe I didn't, but I didn't hold it against her. Also, I didn't want her to let go just yet.

What's it mean? Vi asked.

Is it because of the not-divorce? I asked, because it's what I was thinking about at that exact moment, and I was trying to be more direct.

The not-divorce was something we'd just learned about the day before. What happened was that we were having dinner, vegetarian meatloaf with brussels sprouts and french fries (because our father was willing to eat Brussels sprouts only when they were accompanied by heavily salted french fries, a position I shared), and I had just popped three or twelve french fries into my mouth when my father said that he just wanted us girls to know that there was not going to be a divorce.

Was that, said Vi, on the table?

I didn't say anything because I was chewing maybe fourteen french fries and trying to swallow another half-dozen that were stuck in my throat. But I moved my mouth as if I was also saying something thoughtful.

We kept it from you girls, said our mother. That it was an option, I mean.

But the point is that it's not going to happen, said our father.

Why? asked Vi.

Why what?

Why isn't it going to happen?

Because we're going to plow ahead, said our father. So there's nothing to worry about. Family is everything. The important thing is that we're still intact.

I'm glad, I said. I'd finally swallowed all the french fries. My chest hurt a little because all my saliva had dried up, but at least I could speak and contribute.

But what made you decide to plow ahead? asked Vi.

Because of memories, our mother said, sharing a look with our father that was, I think, supposed to be meaningful and intimate. But they rarely shared looks any longer, and hadn't for as long as I could remember, and so it appeared as if they were two strangers in a bus station who had just discovered, for example, a shared interest in backgammon, or murder.

We've had too many good memories, our father said. We don't want to lose them.

Would we, though? asked Vi.

Probably, he said. He explained that when people get divorced, everything is tainted when you look back on it. Even the loveliest memories, he said, start to curdle when you look back through the prism of unhappiness and regret. And eventually it would seem as if we'd never been happy, and everything had only been a terrible waste of time. The happiness in our past will have been stolen from our present and future selves, he said.

I asked what a prism was.

It just seems, Vi said, like maybe we didn't need to hear this?

We thought you should know, our mother said. Just in case things start to seem a little off.

Feels like things are already a little off, said Vi.

The point is that we still have our memories, our father said. He clapped his hands together, which is what he does to signal that everything is resolved to everyone's satisfaction, and then went off to the shed to spend time with his collection of desiccated butterflies.

The next day, our mother turned see-through.

Unrelated, our father said, when we had dinner that night. The one thing has nothing to do with the other.

Hmm, said Vi. Why do you look smaller?

It was true. Normally our father was a full, slightly balding head taller than our mother when we were sitting together at the table. Now the top of her partly translucent head was about level with his nose, as if he'd slid down a few inches in his chair, the way a child might. And he wasn't only shorter. There seemed to be just a tiny bit less of him, every part of him, as if we'd snapped a family picture when he was standing a few feet behind everyone else, so he wasn't quite to scale.

He frowned at the top of our mother's head, as if perhaps it was to blame. Maybe the rest of you grew, he suggested.

I ran to get the tape measure, and then Vi recorded all our heights on the back of an old Pilates schedule.

Two inches, our father said, as we sat back down. People do get smaller as they age.

Two and a half, I said.

The point is, we shouldn't worry, he said. We're intact, I promise. The family abides. We endure.

It really isn't that bad, our mother said, blinking cheerfully at Vi and at me. She'd been in good spirits all evening even though she found it was harder, now, to lift things and open doors and so forth. She said, You both look lovely tonight, by the way. Really lovely.

I beamed. Vi was in her usual sweats and I had on a chocolate-stained T-shirt from last year's band camp, and neither of us had brushed our hair in three days.

We should do something together after dinner, our father said. Like we used to. As a family. Didn't we used to play games together?

I'm sure we did, our mother said.

Was it *Monopoly*?

Not *Monopoly*, I said, quickly.

The money's all gone, said Vi, and the only piece left is the shoe. And the board is ripped in half.

Only because you guys had too much wine, I said. That one time!

Our father appeared, to me, to shrink just the tiniest bit more in his chair.

Something else then, he said. A walk. How about a walk around the neighborhood? Like we used to.

Okay, I said. I didn't remember us taking walks together, but I remembered other families doing it, and it always looked fun to me. It made me think of families of ducks who walked along together and crossed roads together and protected one another.

We waited until it was growing dark so my mother wouldn't have to explain to the neighbors why she was becoming invisible, and my father wouldn't have to explain why he wasn't to scale anymore. Vi and I walked behind. Our father, now more or less the same size as our mother, reached out to take her very slightly larger hand.

I think they've gone mad, Vi whispered.

Quack, I whispered back.

Streetlamps hummed to life as we walked past. It was warm and windy and the night trees were lit with fireflies. I'd never seen so many. I took Vi's hand and squeezed it.

Hey, she said, and she stopped to look down at our two hands.

What? I asked.

You feel weird. Do I feel weird?

She'd stopped in front of me, and I realized I could see the pale outline of the sidewalk right through her body. But she was glowing, too. Just here and there at first, these pulses of soft white light along her arms, her legs, her cheeks. But more and more appeared as I watched. I wondered if it might be her soul that I was seeing, if she'd been turned inside out somehow, which made me think of exoskeletons, and butterflies. I knew butterflies had exoskeletons to keep safe the soft parts inside. Our father had told us about them.

Why are you crying? she said.

Why do I do anything, I said. Because I didn't know how to tell her about exoskeletons.

Look, she said, pointing down at the sidewalk, where my tears had fallen. They'd formed a puddle on the asphalt, and in the puddle we saw what looked like the twinkling of a thousand stars. They flashed brightly for a few seconds, little supernovas of grief, and then went dark.

The next morning, our father was no more than four feet tall. He looked normal otherwise, though he was dressed now in a pair of Vi's T-ball pants and one of my old SpongeBob T-shirts, which hung on him like a small nightgown. He was using both hands to hold a mug of coffee while our mother, sitting across from him, slid an entire piece of chocolate cake into her mouth.

You're eating cake for breakfast, I said.

You're eating *cake*, Vi said.

I weighed twelve pounds today, our mother said.

Carpe diem! our father said.

We can't have much longer, Vi said. She ran a hand gently along her arm, stirring up a cloud of silver-gold stardust.

Let's not worry, our father said. His voice was fainter now, shrinking along with the rest of him, as if we were hearing him from another room. Let's not lose this chance, he said, to be together.

I've been dreaming that we live somewhere else, Vi said.

Dreams are interesting, our father agreed.

We were living with Mom, not with you.

Well, he said.

We were in the city, in an apartment. I knew it was our place because that clock was on the wall, the one with a face that's half moon and half sun. And we had a dog.

Your mother doesn't like dogs, he said, frowning now into his mug.

I said nothing. But I knew that the dog's name was Daisy, and Vi's room was pale blue, and mine was pale purple with dark purple stenciled clouds up near the ceiling.

I'm going to the shed, our father said.

Wait, I said. Stay. We won't talk about it.

He waved this away with his little hand. I just need to check on something, he said. In the shed.

Your butterflies, I said. They're still there.

Let him go, our mother said.

Our father slid down off the chair and stomped to the sliding door that led to the backyard. With great effort he was able to open the door and slip out into the yard.

We can sit together and talk, our mother said, drifting, almost floating, to the couch. Just the three of us girls. Like we used to. Remember?

I wanted to remember. I wanted to sit with her and with Vi even if there was nothing to remember. But I was watching my father from the window. He'd made it at last to the shed, and he must've shrunk a little more on the way from the house because he couldn't quite reach the door handle. So I went to help him.

The shed was in the back corner of the yard, shaded by hickory trees. Our father built it himself when we first moved into the house. Outside, it looked just like our real house: it was painted white, with flower boxes beneath the windows, and a gabled roof, and a bright yellow door. It even had its own mailbox on a post outside the front door, an exact replica of our real mailbox except three-quarter size. Every day when I was younger, our mother would remove all of our father's mail from the main mailbox, carry it out to the backyard, place it inside his special mailbox, and lift the little red mailbox flag to let him know he had mail. He'd come home from work and look out the window into the yard and see the red flag, and he'd smile his slow quiet smile and then he'd laugh, and she'd laugh, and then he'd go and pick up his mail and read it in his shed before dinner. Then one day I noticed that she left his mail on the island with the rest of the mail, and the little red flag never went up again.

I can't do it, he said now, and his tiny shoulders sagged. He was no taller than my knee.

I put my hand on the door handle. I hadn't been inside in years. He never said we couldn't come in, but he was careful not to ever really invite us either. Sometimes our mother sent one of us out to fetch him, or to ask him a question. We'd stay for a minute or two, bouncing on our heels and sneaking glances at his books, at the old illustrated diagrams that hung from the walls (Insects Harmful and Useful, Conspicuous Beetles of New England, Visual Taxonomy of *Cicindela puritana*), and especially at the butterfly case that hung on the back wall, away from the sunlight that filtered through the hickory branches in through the two small windows. When it was time for us to leave, he'd say jokingly, You'll have to come for a longer visit next time! But we knew he was relieved when we left.

Go on, he said, seeing me hesitate. It's okay.

It was cool inside and there wasn't much furniture: a simple desk, a chair, and an old green loveseat that he'd found on the side of the road and wanted because, at the time, we had a regular-sized green sofa in our living room.

The butterfly case hung on the wall behind the desk, but he was too short now to be able to see it clearly.

Maybe you could take it down for me, he said.

So I removed it from the wall and set it down on the rug. The case was about four feet wide and almost as tall, and there were, I guessed, close to a hundred butterflies pinned behind the glass. Some big ones were scattered here and there—pretty blacks with pearly-white dots along the wing bottoms, iridescent blues tinged with orange specks, one big orange monarch in the bottom right corner that looked like a setting sun about to disappear around the corner of the frame. But most were smaller. And most looked, to me, like the same butterfly, of palest blue outlined in white, with flecks of black and brown along the wing tips.

What's this one? I asked.

Spring azure, he said. *Celastrina ladon.*

Is it rare?

Common, he said. They were everywhere when I was growing up.

I asked why he'd kept so many, then.

Because they were his favorite, he said.

Whose favorite?

He put his hand, which was now about the size of a cat's paw, on the glass. Well, he said. You had an uncle, I guess.

You guess?

He cleared his throat and said, He wasn't an uncle then. He would've been an uncle. He died long ago. An accident. I was there, too.

Why don't we know about him?

We never spoke of him. They never did, I mean, so I never did either. Too sad. Nobody wanted to be sad.

You were *there?*

He was so little, he said. Even for his age. And he couldn't see anything. Thick glasses, near-sighted. But he loved bugs, and microscopes. So he could see things no one else could see.

What was his name? I asked.

Adam, he said.

I'm sorry.

Well. You know. It was so long ago.

My skin was mostly transparent, now, dark and pulsating with its new weird light. I laid my hand on the glass beside his. I always wanted to touch their wings, I said. When we came to visit here.

I didn't know, he said.

It hurt me sometimes, I said. Not to touch them.

He turned to look up at me, at the giant face of his daughter. Go on, he said.

Won't it fall apart if I touch it?

Try, he said.

So I lifted free the glass case and set it aside. Then I knelt on the floor with my knees touching the wood frame, and leaned forward to touch one of the smallest of the pale blue azures.

It's still soft, I marveled.

Then its wings fluttered.

We both sat back on our heels. The pins which kept the butterfly in place slipped free, and the azure rose from the case, wings beating ponderously for a few seconds. But it steadied itself and flapped harder, rising and falling and darting madly, left and right, as if caught up in a current. Learning to fly, to be alive again. Then it made its way to the open doorway, and flew off.

We looked at each other.

The rest, he said. Quickly.

You're sure?

I'm sure, he said.

So I touched each butterfly in turn, and each broke free and took flight. In less than a minute the room was a cloud of resurrected butterflies, and we lay on our backs to watch them, his small hand in mine.

Once they'd all flown at last through the open door, he climbed into the case and lay on his back. He was about the size now of a large dragonfly. He stretched his arms wide.

I'm not going to pin you, I said.

It's not so bad, he said. I could get used to it.

The days passed.

Some days I awoke in a purple room with purple clouds near the ceiling, and outside the window was a quiet, leafy city street. I watched the leaves blow about as I walked to school with Vi, a new denim backpack slung over my shoulder, and I thought of the way the leaves sounded underfoot, *crunch whisper whisper crunch*, and I thought of Susie, the girl who sat next to me in Social Studies, who I wanted as a friend because she'd drawn dancing skeletons on all her book covers. Some days I awoke and I was made of stars, and Vi was made of stars. Our mother was so light that we had to tie a string to her to keep her from floating up and out the window. Our father was small enough that we worried we'd squash him if he were left free to roam, so we brought the Christmas village down from the attic and set it up in front of the bay window, and we moved him into the Alpine Lodge. We tried to be together.

But I think it won't be long, now.

Some days I can't quite remember what I think I'm supposed to remember. It's all a little mixed up in my head, me and not-me. The one who sleeps in a different place now.

I feel like I'm forgetting things, I tell Vi. We're almost to school. The weather is getting cooler now, even in the city. I'm still wearing only a zip-up hoodie, the one that's not mine. Our father gave it to me the last time we stayed with him, because I'd packed only T-shirts for the weekend. I'll buy you one to keep here, he said. No, this one is good, I said. I like the way it smells.

Which things, says Vi. Checking her phone, which is in a black case printed with the words "Gothic Babe" in silver gothic letters.

(A moving truck has appeared outside our house. It's late afternoon on a fall day. I know it's fall because the hickory trees in the backyard have started dropping their yellow leaves, and no one has swept them away. I wonder where the summer went.)

I don't know, I tell Vi. From when we were together. What it was like.

Watch this, she says, and hands me her phone, and I watch a video of a baby panda sliding down a muddy slope.

(Another family moves in, and we watch them settle in: a young couple with a baby, just starting out. They don't notice us. We're someone else's memories, that's all. The house fills quickly with their things, their sounds, their wholeness. We pack up the Christmas Village, and secure our mother, and we go out to the backyard.)

I think it was good, I say. Wasn't it good?

(Like we're camping again, our father says, as we lie side by side in the leaf-covered grass under the early evening sky.)

(We never camped, says Vi.)

(We almost did, that one time. We talked about it, anyway. Hold on to your mother, now.)

I'm sitting at my school desk by the window, and rain beats quietly against the glass. It makes me think of butterflies, and I wonder what they do, what they feel, when it rains. If they know their wings can still beat, or if they worry that it will be too much for them. If it will be more than they can take.

(Clouds are gathering overhead. I feel a tug inside me. Something small and maybe important breaks loose from the left side of my chest. I put my hand over the spot, as if to keep it inside, whatever it is that's broken loose. I see a plume of silver dust swirling up through my fingers, rising toward the sky.)

(Hey, I say.)

Hey, I say, taking a breath as I lean toward Susie. I really like your dancing skeletons.

(Is it now? asks Vi.)

(Take Mom's hand, I say. I've got Dad.)

I could teach you to draw them sometime, she says. If you want. You're new here, right?

Yes, I say, and yes. I mean I am, yes, and I'd like that.

(I'm here, says our mother.)

(I'm not ready, says our father.)

(We're okay, I say.)

I turn to look out the window again. I think of the azures, the ones that were alive when our father was a boy, years ago. They didn't have much time here. Only four or five days. Not as long as the uncle I never knew. But longer than my cousin Ainsley. Long enough to learn their way around, and to feel their wings warmed by the sunlight, and to be thrown about by the wind and the rain, and certainly to die. Long enough to leave something behind to be collected, and loved, and remembered. Like me.

Homecoming

MEZIL CALLED NO ONE when he landed, as he'd been instructed.

He spent the night at a roadside motel outside Hartford, waking every half hour to street sounds and a red vacancy sign blinking through the thin drapes, then rolling before dawn on the first of three buses home, dressed in civilian clothes. The instructions had arrived the day before he left Saigon, typewritten, no signature, no return address except *Covington, CT*. Mezil read it a dozen times, lying in his bunk, and understood none of it. Yet here he was, *arriving in the morning*, dressed *not as a soldier*, and *limiting his contact with others*. In fact he'd spoken only one word since landing at Bradley, and that was to the motel clerk, a kid Mezil's age who had signed him in and handed him the key, and then looked at Mezil in his uniform—whippet-thin Mezil, whose uniform hung on him like an older brother's suit handed down too soon—and asked him a question.

The sun was up by the time he reached Covington. He stepped out, lugging a duffel bag as long as Mezil himself and twice as wide, into a cold weekday morning in November.

Walk home from the station alone.

Another easy one, as it turned out. He'd forgotten how small Covington was. Small enough to walk edge to edge in forty-five minutes, and small enough that the people he saw as he left the station should've recognized him. Should've, maybe, offered him a ride home, or at least joined him for a block or two. Wasn't that Rosecki's mom coming out of Dale's pharmacy across the street? And wasn't that Mr. Garvey, his shop teacher in high school, waiting at the stop light in the same rusted orange pickup truck he'd used to drive Mezil to the doctor after Mezil passed out from turpentine fumes and cracked his head on the floor? (*How many fingers, Mezil*, and Mezil said he thought maybe eleven or twelve, and Mr. Garvey said *Well, which one is it, eleven or twelve?*) They seemed to sneak glances at him now, only for their eyes to skate over him when he turned back to look, and what madness was that?

But it was all madness now, and he didn't know what to make of it, any of it. Maybe he looked different, unrecognizable. Maybe he wasn't really here.

He turned a corner, lowering his head as he moved past a young girl in ripped bell-bottom jeans and a Red Sox cap, straddling a bike.

"Mezil," she said, clear and bright as day. It was only then, Mezil's soul jumping clear through his body, that he realized with how much certainty he'd become convinced that he was dead.

"You grew," he said.

"Well, I worked at it." She cocked her head, sizing him up, which made him want to look away.

"How's Mookie?" Though Mezil and her brother had been born two days apart, Mezil had drawn 45, the other boy 310.

"Dumb," she said. "Wrecked his moped a couple weeks back and broke his wrist."

"Same, then." Mezil looked around, rubbed his mostly nonexistent whiskers. Then, turning back to the girl: "Not sure you're supposed to talk to me."

"Yeah, I know." She pulled down the brim of the cap, which almost made him smile. She appraised him again, and he tried not to think of what she was imagining, what measure he was falling short of for this thirteen-year-old girl with whom he'd played endless games of *Battleship* and *Sorry!* on Saturday mornings, waiting for Mookie to wake the hell up.

She lifted her shoulders and gripped the handlebars, and with the faintest smile said, "Now as you were, Mezil." And she took off down the street into the wind, ponytail bobbing, before he could think to answer.

BUT HE CAN'T *be a soldier*, is what Mezil's mother had said to his father.

That was after Roger Mudd preempted *Mayberry R.F.D.* and they'd all watched Mezil's number come up on a blue capsule, after Mezil said what does it mean and his father said Well, and then they all dispersed for a while to their different secret places to make sense of it all, Mezil's being his bedroom closet with a copy of the inaugural issue of *From Beyond the*

Unknown, featuring the Turtle-Men from Mars. It was after he listened to the entire *Revolver* album, twice. It was after the lights went out and his parents went to bed, when Mezil listened through the thin walls of the house as they discussed what would become of their only son.

He'll be okay, from Mezil's father, who didn't sound to Mezil as if he totally believed it.

Can he even lift a gun? from his mother, which, okay, might've stung a bit, except that Mezil had been wondering the same thing.

He'll learn.

And if he doesn't? If he's the worst soldier who ever lived? Then what?

This was something Mezil hadn't even considered himself until that moment. Mezil's father said only, *He'll make it back.*

But as it turned out, Mezil wasn't the worst solder who ever lived, or even the worst soldier in his squad.

That was Boone.

Boone at least looked like a soldier. He was big, half a foot taller than Mezil, and as thick as a defensive lineman. Blond-haired and blue-eyed with a peach-fuzz blond beard, he was saved from being too good-looking by an asymmetrical face—the left ear hanging down a little low, something not quite right happening with the spacing of his eyes, a broken nose that had been reset without much attention to detail or aesthetics. Early on, the word everyone used to describe him, a word no one would have thought to use about Mezil, was *solid*. They meant not only his physique but his demeanor. They meant he looked rugged, reliable, brave, probably a little dumb, obedient, and plain-spoken, all qualities held in high regard. Country Boy, they called him, because they all had to have nicknames, and everyone including Mezil assumed that's what he was.

But Boone was none of those things. He wasn't even a country boy. He'd grown up in West Orange, New Jersey, the son of a great bearded giant who ran a flower shop called Rose & Thorn. By the time he was drafted, Boone had never thrown a football or hit a baseball in his life, but he could name all hundred and fifty species of roses. He could recite Rilke's *Duino Elegies* in the original German by heart, though he understood no German. He was near-sighted. He was gentle like his father, and sensitive, and unguarded. He hated violence, as a matter of basic temperament rather than principle. He was, most damningly, *soft*.

Of course they'd all been soft. Wherever they'd been raised, whatever nicknames they'd adopted or had chosen for themselves, however far their souls had traveled and whatever damage sustained on the road from then to now. Even Fragman, who slept with a finger tucked through a grenade pin and kept a pet rat the size of a housecat, and Big Todd, who'd greeted Mezil on his first day by showing him a cigar box filled with human tongues—*These weren't all mine, but I feel like I need them anyway*—had been soft once, or so Mezil wanted to believe. It was just that PFC Boone didn't seem likely to live long enough to harden himself. He was a terrible shot. He had a maddening tendency to wander off course when they were out on patrol. He was a compulsive daydreamer. He was clumsy, distracted, heavy-footed and forgetful. If there were a secret checklist for the least desirable qualities in a soldier (and Mezil felt sure there was just such a checklist) then PFC Boone would have had every box checked, with a few extra items jotted on the back of the list, furiously underlined.

"Two months," Fragman pronounced one July morning, a couple weeks after Boone arrived.

"Two months for what?" Mezil asked.

"The Ghost," he said.

Behind Boone's back the others had taken to calling him Ghost, because in their minds he was already gone. In Vietnam there was always a Ghost, and in their unit it was Boone. Two months meant two months until he got his head blown off by a sniper, or stepped on a punji stick and developed sepsis, or tripped a landmine. Wanting nothing to do with the dead, they avoided him at meals, stopped smoking with him, stopped asking him questions, stopped answering questions beyond grunts and monosyllables. There was no malice in it. Some of them had been in-country for months and were counting their days. All of them, even Mezil, had lived through battles, or things that weren't battles but worse, things that had no name they'd ever learned. They all carried memories of places and stories in which they'd played no role, Quảng Ngãi and My Lai and Huế and the A Shau Valley, which through the retelling or the careful non-telling had become as real as their own memories, so that when Big Todd spoke of the fog burning away from the Song Ve Valley despite never having set foot there, never having spoken to anyone who had set foot there, they all understood, because they all remembered it too, they all could feel on their skin the coolness of the vanishing fog and hear the shorebirds from the distant surf of the South China Sea. Boone, somehow, didn't remember, and the rest of them had forgotten what it was like to not remember. A Ghost with only his own memories was no use to any of them.

Mezil understood all of this. He understood that Boone was a threat to his, Mezil's, mental and physical well-being, and that he had to keep his distance from Boone like the others, the same way he'd keep his distance from a nest of bamboo pit vipers.

The problem was that he liked Boone.

The problem was that for no reason he could understand, he found Boone—graceless, inappropriate, goofy, not-long-for-this-world Boone—kind of wonderful.

"I'd like to talk about robots now," Boone would say, at one in the morning, turning to face Mezil's bunk. "I have some reservations."

And Mezil would tell him to fuck off. Because it was one in the morning, and because he already knew everything there was to know, by now, about Boone's reservations about robots.

Or: "I've been thinking a lot about the end of *Hamlet.*"

Or: "I think I should tell you now about my father's beard."

Or: "I have a theory about golems. Not the one I told you already, but a different one."

It was always like that. Always late at night, always something Boone had been thinking about, worrying about, chewing over, and he just thought Mezil needed to hear. Not that Mezil wanted to hear, but that he *needed* to hear, or at least Boone needed to tell him. And always Mezil said the same thing: Fuck off, Boone. Even if a part of him was curious, too, about the thousand-year-old wild dog rose that grew in Germany, or worried that the North Star wouldn't be the North Star in 13,000 years because there would be another North Star by then, he'd keep it to himself, he'd pretend to fall back asleep. Boone would continue talking anyway, and Mezil would eventually fall asleep for real, to Boone's voice. Was there, maybe, a part of him that liked falling asleep to Boone's voice? That took comfort in it? He didn't know, any more than he knew why Boone had picked him in the first place, other than the proximity of their bunks.

One night Mezil found on his pillow the torn-out bottom square of a box of C-Rations (ham and lima beans), on which Boone had drawn a surprisingly good three-panel comic strip about a pair of soldiers named Meeks and Basil. In the strip, Basil, oversized and hunch-shouldered and prone to daydreaming, is about to step on a punji stick trap when he's saved by the wiry, courageous Meeks, in the process sending them both tumbling down a comically big hill into the brush, where they land in a heap of tangled limbs. *Well that was a close one,* says Basil in the last panel, sitting atop

Meeks, oblivious to the nest of vipers waking up beside them both. Mezil tore the strip to pieces and tossed the pieces on Boone's bunk.

Next day there was another in its place. And the next day, another. Always it was Basil getting into some ridiculous scrape, his head in the clouds, mostly unaware of the danger even after it had passed, like Mr. Magoo, while the ever-resourceful and ever-courageous Meeks kept him out of harm's way.

In one strip, at the end, the two of them sit apart in a field under a jungle of stars, Basil on the left and Meeks on the right, their heads tilted up to watch a Huey copter glide past in the dark.

Thanks, Meeks, says the bubble over Basil's head.

Fuck off, Basil, says the bubble over Meeks's head.

Mezil stopped throwing them away. But he never acknowledged them, either. They worried him, like everything worried him, and he fought against his own instincts toward kindness. He and Boone weren't friends. They couldn't be friends, because Mezil wanted to survive, wanted to go back home to Covington, wanted to be upstairs in his bedroom with *From Beyond the Unknown*. He could see it when he closed his eyes. It wasn't much, as visions went, and he hoped that its smallness kept it in reach. He could safeguard that much. He could protect something as small as that. But no more than that. There wasn't room in the vision for Boone.

And then Boone would say, "My father's beard," and quietly hand Mezil a drawing of a disembodied beard.

Once, Mezil slipped. He said something about meeting up for a beer when they made it back home. Boone shrugged it off quietly and changed the subject. And it occurred to Mezil, then, that maybe Boone wasn't so oblivious. That maybe the reason he talked to Mezil the way he did was that he knew he was a Ghost, and he didn't want all he had and all he was to be lost with him. Maybe that's all it was.

Mezil walked by Harry's Bait and Tackle as somewhere behind him a car backfired. He turned off the main road and slipped down a side street painted with orange and yellow leaves, keeping his head down.

He was thinking of how Boone had confided one night that he had a suspicion he couldn't quite shake. Because of a dream, he said. In the dream they were sending him home from Vietnam. The catch was that he had to leave behind a copy of himself. That's just how it worked, in Boone's dream, if you wanted to go home. He could go back to West Orange and the flower shop and his father and his books, and he could try to build some humble little life for himself there. But there would always be this other Boone he'd left behind. And this other Boone, the left-behind Boone, would never know. He'd never remember or suspect that he was only a copy, that it was his job to stay and fight, and lose faith, and get dysentery, and question his purpose, and see horrible things, and maybe do horrible things. This other Boone would have trouble remembering who he was before. With each passing day, his memories would degrade a little more, until finally he'd have no recollection at all of who he'd been. He'd be too far removed from the real Boone, the original Boone, to even be considered Boone anymore. And someday, a week or a month or a year down the road, this other Boone, this degraded copy, would die. All so the real Boone could move on with his quiet, safe little life. That's the bargain, Boone told Mezil, that you're asked to take when you want to go home. And Mezil said, blinking at him in the dark, forgetting that he was pretending to be asleep: So you have a terrible suspicion you'd take the bargain. And Boone said, No. I have a terrible suspicion the real Boone did.

What was it like to kill someone over there? That's what the motel clerk had asked.

Mezil had thought about it, tried to make sense of the question. When he opened his mouth to speak he had no idea what he was about to say, and it was only one word, and the word was *Easy.*

He lifted his head, now, as he came to his parents' street. Not his street anymore. His parents' street. He reached into his pocket and unfolded the instructions. The wind rattled the paper as he read the last line.

Come to the Tavern at Eight. And be ready.

Ready. What could that even mean? What could they want that he, Mezil, could possibly give them?

BY SEVEN-THIRTY Mickey—who'd inherited the Tavern from his mother, widowed at thirty-five with four children, blessed to her great surprise with a natural talent for calculating probabilities and calling the bluff of overconfident drunks at the card table—finally succeeded in getting a healthy fire going. The process was fraught enough with suspense to set off among the fifty or so men and women assembled in the tavern a semi-drunken and profane chorus of "For He's a Jolly Good Fellow." Which was an improvement, anyway, on earlier, mangled versions of "Down Among the Dead

Men" and "Barnacle Bill." Mickey took a bow and someone passed him a pint of beer, which he downed in one long gulp, raising another cheer.

The tavern was dark, as always, not so much an aesthetic choice on Mickey's part as an economic one, though in this case, by tradition, a few extra bulbs had been left unlit. Supplemental candlelight lent the room a softer, mid-century glow, if the century happened to be the eighteenth rather than twentieth. In the center of the main room they'd cleared all the tables and installed a wooden platform, eight feet to a side, on which sat a single upholstered armchair borrowed from the back room where Mickey used it the rest of the time for midafternoon naps.

More people arrived, some by the front door but most by the back. They came alone and in groups, couples and old men and war widows, teachers and housewives and postmen and auto mechanics, some of whom knew the inside of Mickey's better than others. No one under thirty was technically invited or allowed, but security was lax enough that a twelve-year-old girl in ripped bell-bottom jeans and a Red Sox cap could make her way inside and find a spot tucked away in the shadows, and score a root beer in a frosted glass, with only a bit of attitude.

The noise level in the room grew as the hour approached and the last of the stragglers filtered in, shivering against the day and the decade. Mickey's fire roared on.

At eight o'clock the door creaked open, and the room fell silent as Mezil, the boy, stepped inside.

He pushed the door closed and then, seemingly defeated, took them all in. It was too dark for him to make out their faces. He looked small and uncertain, but in the tilt of his head he was defiant too. For a moment they thought he might turn and disappear through the door into the windy night, and for that moment he thought the same. But then he stepped forward, and made his way to the chair.

A kind of collective sigh filled the room when he sat down. Everyone shifted, getting comfortable, murmuring quietly but enthusiastically, emptying or refilling their glasses. Meanwhile Mezil sat with his body straight and tense against the padded chair. Waiting for it to begin, perhaps, so that it could end.

The old chief of police, Carver, was the first to break the silence, from the shadows along the back wall. He cleared his throat apologetically, not having many opportunities for public speaking these days, and said, "This was in, I don't know, '57 or '58. Found Mezil out behind Mac's garage when he wasn't five years old yet. Burying a hamster. Told me he'd seen something sparkling on the hill behind the garage, all the way from his bedroom window. Just junk metal glinting in the sunlight was all it was. But Mezil thought it'd be a nice place, I guess. Anyways he stuffed the rat in a plastic bag and dragged it all the way through town. Set us all chasing after him, you remember." Some nods at this, and a few affectionate eye-rolls. "I yelled at him good and told him he'd have to spend the night in jail for trespassing or such. Just scaring him so he'd use his head next time. Drove him home with the lights flashing, him sobbing like a loon and clutching the plastic shovel he brought with him for Willis—that was the rat's name. He named the rat Willis. So, anyways, I sent him running back into his house where Faye was waiting for him. Then I guess I went back and finished burying the rat. Figured I had to."

Next was Rosicky's mom. She talked about how she'd sit by the window drinking her coffee in the morning after Rosicky left for school, watching the kids pass by the house. And Mezil would do this thing, she said—it wasn't exactly a dance, at least not like a regular human person dance. More like electrical spasms? He'd jump into the air, spin, jump backward, shoot his arms into the air, freeze, spin again, jump forward, freeze, crouch, spin a third time—like something was jolting him with these little bursts of electric joy. It didn't happen all the time, she said. Only when no one else was around, and only for that little stretch of sidewalk in front of her house. The rest of the time he was quiet, you could tell he was quiet. You'd never know all that was inside him, said Rosicky's mom.

Mezil's mother and father spoke then, about Mezil the Wolf. Mezil went through a phase, at six years old, when he thought he was a wolf. A quiet, solitary boy, he'd always pretended to be other things—an Egyptian mummy swathed in Ace bandages for entire weekends, a willow tree who could communicate only by waving its arms, and who needed maple syrup to survive—so it didn't seem out of character when he took to howling, and loping around the backyard on all fours, and licking his arms to groom himself. He took to sleeping in his closet surrounded by his pack, a motley collection of stuffed wolves, bears, tigers, and one gray owl with a Band-Aid across its left eye. For weeks it went like that. Each night before bed he was allowed outside for an hour, and he spent the time prowling restlessly in the yard, his howl growing more animal-like as the days stretched on, more melancholy. Finally one night she found him back in his bed, his face tear-streaked, and when she asked him what had happened he said that they hadn't come. He said he was supposed to have forty-two teeth and he'd howled every day but they hadn't come, and so he knew, then, that the rest of it wouldn't come either, and he would never rejoin his pack, and he would only ever be who and what he was. So she called Mezil's father into the bedroom and shut off the light, and the three of them lay together in the bed and howled quietly at the dark and the moon, until they slept.

One after another, people took the floor and told stories. Mezil himself dropped his head, but he listened to them talk. Everyone seemed to have a story, however brief, however glancingly it alighted on Mezil himself. About things he'd said or an impression he'd made, about his awkwardness and his shyness and his touching, oddball decency. From there the conversation turned to the war, not this particular war but The War, endless and capitalized and monolithic. The older men in the room, and many of the women, shared their own stories. They spoke of hiding, and marching, and sitting in boredom, and waiting in trenches, and dreaming of home, and singing and telling jokes, and of killing and seeing those who were killed. They spoke of how it looked—how the world looked—when you came home after all of that, how *they* were looked at and how they looked at themselves, what it meant to be alive when so many were dead, how terrible it was to still be alive, how terrible to be glad to be alive and coming home, when all they ever wanted was home, all they dreamt of was home, all that ever mattered, for all of them, but also for those they fought and killed, was finding their way home.

When the stories ended, Mezil raised his head. He understood that he'd been wrong. That they weren't and had never been waiting for him to speak. Nothing was asked of him, nothing demanded. He could stay quiet and it would be okay. They'd understand, and they'd know why he was silent, and it would be okay.

"I'd like to talk," he said, "about Boone."

And so they heard about Country Boy, the Ghost, the worst soldier in Mezil's unit, the son of a florist from New Jersey. They heard about the hundred and fifty species of roses, and Boone's reservations about robots, and his two theories about golems, and the adventures of Basil and Meeks. They heard about Boone's father's beard. And when there was nothing left but for Mezil to tell it, they heard about the day Boone wandered off course on patrol, and Mezil—thoughtful, decent Mezil, who dragged his hamster Willis across town to bury him, and who danced like a mad dervish on his way to school for no reason except that he was excited to be alive—just let him go. Let him wander off, like a bothersome dog. Because that day he was angry at Boone's soft and terrible heart, because he wanted to help Boone become a better soldier and stay alive, because he'd overheard the others talking when they thought he was asleep, heard them say the word *Ghost*. Only they weren't talking about Boone this time, they were talking about Mezil. So he let Boone disappear behind him. He'll learn, Mezil thought, and make it back—or he won't. Mezil couldn't be responsible. He was responsible for protecting only his one small fragile space, not the wider space that included Boone or anyone else.

In the morning they found him. His hands and feet nailed to a tree, his dog tags hanging from the big toe of his right foot. They found his head not far from a village they'd passed through only days before. Of course the villagers denied everything, the problem being that the guilty would deny it, too. Whether what happened was driven by vengeance for Boone's death, or guilt for their role in it, or whether those things were only justifications for some darker impulse, Mezil never knew. Mezil himself killed only a few of them. But it was Mezil—the others all agreed, afterward—it was quiet, thoughtful, decent Mezil who was the most savage of them all. Someone carved a new nickname into the wall above his bunk, as a tribute. MEZIL THE MERCILESS, in letters six inches high, jagged as shark's teeth.

He slumped then in his chair, head down, tired and lost in himself. His thin body shook quietly, though he made no sound. Meanwhile the fire crackled in the hearth and those in the room looked on, waiting. Eventually the shaking subsided. Mezil's breathing slowed and his shoulders relaxed. His head fell forward, his eyes drooped. In minutes he was asleep.

"Orderly fashion," said Mickey.

One by one they approached. Mothers and fathers, neighbors, teachers and priests, men and women who had lost their own sons or worried for their own sons, they broke free from the shadows and stepped up onto the platform. A few leaned down to whisper things to the sleeping Mezil, confiding secrets, making promises, offering mea culpas. Most said nothing. They touched the top of his sleeping head, or rested a hand on his shoulder, and then walked away. In the end Mezil's father came forward with two other men, and they lifted Mezil out of the chair. They carried him to a back room where a bed had been made up. Then they returned to the bar to settle in with the others, and keep watch.

Metamorphosis

ONE DAY THE MAN noticed that his eyes, after being brown his whole life, were now green. A muted green, and still with some brown around the pupil, but definitely green. It was interesting. His first thought was to tell his wife, because she was always the one he told whenever something interesting happened, but she was dying, and he thought she wouldn't want to hear about it.

Technically she was in the Early Stage of dying, according to the nurse who came to the house each morning. There would be a Middle Stage and then a Last Stage. In the Early Stage, she was restless and fatigued and uncomfortable, and her lips were too dry, and she was losing her appetite, but she was still able to talk. She still *wanted* to talk. So he could've brought up the eye thing. It's just that she didn't want to talk about current events, such as eye things. She didn't want to talk about things that were going to keep going, keep happening, after she was gone. She wanted only to talk about old things.

Which he totally got, and it was fine, he understood. Really. It just would've been nice if the old things she wanted to talk about included both of them.

For example.

Movies, she said yesterday.

And he, sitting in the armchair facing the bed, brought out his blue notebook, the one he used for her lists. This was a time of lists.

Ready, he said.

Notorious, she said. Bergman. Hitchcock.

This was how she spoke, now, in fragments. Only the essentials.

Sure, he said. A classic. Nazis. Cary Grant. And he wrote *Notorious* in the notebook. Then he underlined it, and put stars next to it, and enclosed one of the stars in a circle. It wasn't that he thought the symbols—there were others, there were exactly six others, and exactly twenty-four allowable combinations—meant anything, or could alter the course of her illness, or.

He didn't think that. But he never skipped them.

And she said, No, with a tired and rather baleful look. Weren't any (deep, annoyed breath) Nazis.

He smiled, reassuringly he hoped, and said, Well. Worrying that she was confused, that she'd moved farther along in the Early Stage than he was prepared for just yet.

Psychologist, she said. Psychiatrist. Whatever.

He brightened and said, *Spellbound*! Relieved that she hadn't gone to the Middle Stage without him. Then: I don't think we saw that one, though. Together, I mean.

No, she said. We didn't.

Which, again: fine. It's just that everything was like this. Everything seemed to be about her, exclusively about her. Always before, it had been about Them.

Of course he knew she'd had a life before they were together, just as he'd had a life. She'd had childhood friends, taken trips in the family station wagon, had crushes and went on dates, gone away to college in New England, lived in New York City for a time. She'd fallen in and out of love several times, he knew, before they ever met. He understood all that. It's just that it worried him that they had to dwell there. In that time. It worried him for reasons he couldn't explain, the way it worried him to see photographs of his parents when they were young, before they'd had him, before they even had each other. As if imagining such things back then meant that choices were still to be made. That things could be different now. And why after all were these the things that she needed to remember now? Why was this where they had to dwell in the last days (the Early Stage of the last days)? They'd laid down roots together, the two of them. They were entangled. He didn't want to become untangled, now, at the end of things.

Still, he decided to keep the eye thing to himself.

She wanted to talk about vacations today. So he took out the blue notebook and wrote *Vacations* at the top of a new page. He was thinking of the last big trip they'd taken before she got sick, which was to Florence. They'd stayed in a small inn not far from the Duomo, and a mosquito had made its way into the room the first night, and then followed them or seemed to follow them everywhere they went. To the shops of Ponte Vecchio and up to the top of Piazzale Michelangelo, and even inside the Uffizi. Their personal tour guide. *Here you will find da Vinci's unfinished* Adoration of the Magi. *Le ombre . . . semplicemente magnifiche. Bzzzzz. . . .* She even gave the mosquito a name, because she liked to name things.

Wildwood beach, she was saying. 1981.

What was the name, he said, of that Italian mosquito?

I took my friend (she stopped, head turned on the pillow, looked out the window, searching). *Rose.* Her name. Write it down.

So he wrote *Wildwood beach, 1981, w/Rose,* and he asked her to tell him about where they stayed (a duplex three blocks from the boardwalk, with an upright piano that was missing a third of the keys), and how the boardwalk smelled (salt air, cigarette smoke, funnel cake, hot grease, vinegar, wet concrete, candle wax, taffy), and what Rose whispered to her the last night of the trip after they'd climbed into bed and shut off the light (only *thank you,* again and again, squeezing her hand in the dark: a mystery).

Later the nurse came, and he went for a walk.

They lived in a town of a few thousand people in the shadows of the Hudson Highlands. The town's claim to fame, if it had one, was the fall Applefest, which drew thirty thousand people from New York and Connecticut every year on the first Sunday in October. There was a maple-tree-lined Main Street and a covered wooden bridge. There were three creameries, and a shop that sold only maple syrup, and another shop that sold only artisanal olive oils. It was small enough that he could walk, during the hour when the nurse was at the house, all the way across town to the college where he (and, once, she) worked, and then back again. Small enough that he saw, mostly, the same faces on the streets each day.

He turned down Main and walked past the maple syrup shop, head down, trying to remember the name of the mosquito that had followed them around in Florence. Luigi, he thought, maybe. Or no, that wasn't quite right. But there was a g, and it had a lot of syllables, because he could remember her drawing the name out, delighted. Giovanni?

No.

He crossed the street (Gustavo, Giancarlo, Georgino, Gilberto, Gerardo) and as he stepped up on the curb, he ran straight into a chain-link fence.

He stepped back, startled. It was a temporary construction fence that had been erected around the corner in both directions. A sign on the fence, beside the building permit, advertised a new three-story "mixed-use commercial and residential property," coming soon. There was an artist's rendering of a pretty but old-fashioned brick building, the bottom floor occupied by a brightly-lit cafe with a yellow and white striped awning.

When was the last time something new had gone up in town? He couldn't remember. He couldn't even remember what used to be here on this corner, or when it had been torn down. A crane and other heavy construction equipment were already visible behind the fence, and as he watched, a construction crew was getting ready to go to work.

He crossed to the other side of the street so he could return to the sidewalk, and then continued on his way, winding through the town. Thinking, still, of the mosquito (Garibaldi?), and of who they used to be. The two of them. In Florence they'd walked ten miles a day. In the rain! All their trips were like that in the old days. It felt good to walk, to learn a new city by feeling it underfoot. He'd always marveled at how wherever they went, she always seemed to know her way. As if she were building each new city as she discovered it. He could get lost even here, even at home.

In fact he was slightly turned around at the moment, so he stopped. He was on a quiet street lined with two-story Cape-Cod-style homes. Wet yellow leaves covered the road and the sidewalk. He knew he must have walked the street dozens of times, but he couldn't recall now precisely where it led. He thought he could see, far ahead, a dense thicket of trees and what looked like the entrance to a park. A pair of young joggers crossed the street and disappeared inside the park as he stood watching.

He turned and looked back the way he'd come. He could still hear the new construction on Main Street, but it sounded distant, as if he'd walked farther than he really had.

Confusing, he thought.

(Middle Stage, he thought.)

He shook his head to clear it, then checked his watch, which hung a bit on his wrist today. Time to get back already. Maybe he'd walked slower than usual.

Was there always a park? he asked his wife, later. They were in the living room. He'd carried her down from the bedroom and set her up in the extra bed, the one they'd arranged by the bay window so she could look out on the street.

I got turned around, he explained.

Hmm, she said, half-closing her eyes. I loved the park. Central. Saturdays in . . . the fall. I'd wake up early, and. . . .

He knew this story. Her first months in New York after college, just starting out in her career, the one she'd had before becoming a teacher, like him. If he was being honest, not his favorite topic of conversation. He thought sometimes of their old lives, before they met, before there was a Them, as being like two novels. His was slim, the spine barely thick enough to support a title. The protagonist spent a lot of time thinking, wondering about things, happily puzzled by the world. There were too many conversations, mostly about books. There were some quiet thrills, yes, and sadnesses and misadventures and even romance, but these were all scaled, it seemed to him, to the small towns in which he'd always lived and gone to school and worked.

Her novel was different. He imagined it as a kind of globe-hopping picaresque, with dozens of major characters and convoluted subplots and tangents that occupied a hundred pages at a time. It was a novel in which the protagonist backpacked across Europe as a teenager, and broke her leg in a motorcycle accident, and organized protest marches in her hometown, and took a job teaching in the city after college, and learned to be a part of the city, to find its rhythms and to let it carry her toward whoever it was she was going to become. It was at a different scale, her story, and nothing seemed larger in his mind than her time in New York, or farther and more different from the life the two of them had now together. Maybe he was intimidated by it. Maybe it was only that he was protective still of their own story, the one that hadn't yet ended.

I know, he said, too abruptly. You woke at dawn, and you went across the street to Ernie's to buy a bagel and coffee, and then you walked to the park, and then.

She said nothing.

I'm sorry, he said. I'm just having some trouble. With this. Looking around at the IV stand, the bed, the pill bottles and letters and notebooks scattered everywhere. The everything-ness of it.

Me too, she said.

It's hard, he said.

Yes, she said.

They were silent for a moment then. He stood beside the bed and they looked together out the window. It was getting dark earlier now, and as they watched, the streetlamp outside their place flickered on.

Did we have a streetlamp before? she asked.

Interesting, he said.

You know, she said. It wasn't Ernie's.

No?

Eddy's, she said.

The next morning, drying off after his shower, he noticed that the hair on his arms and legs and chest was gone. Or not gone, entirely, but what was left was so small and fine and golden that it might as well have been invisible. When the nurse came, he took her aside and asked if he should be worried.

Would you rather have more body hair? she asked. Or less?

Does it have to be one or the other?

Seems that way, she said. Do you feel healthy?

I think so, he said. He actually felt better, physically, than he had in years, which seemed terrible. Under the circumstances.

Main Street was buzzing with life when he went for his walk. So many people, now. Some he knew, but most were strangers. He noticed that they'd installed two new streetlights to handle the pedestrian traffic. The three-story mixed-use construction site was coming along, although he saw from the rendering that they'd updated it to eight stories instead of three. The steel supports for the first five stories were already in place, and dozens of construction workers in orange vests moved about, ascending and descending, voices echoing in the bright air.

He left Main Street. New buildings were going up elsewhere, too, or had already gone up and he'd missed them. It was, he thought, a curious mix. There was a Chinese restaurant announcing its grand opening, and a community theater staging a production of *Twelfth Night*, and a popup shop that sold pizza for only fifty cents a slice, and a basement fortune teller and palm reader, and a gift store that sold lemon-themed gifts (glass lemon Christmas ornaments, lemon-decorated serving bowls and platters, lemon drop earrings, watercolors of lemon trees growing on the cliffs of Positano). On one sidewalk he found an empty kiosk with a sign advertising sunset boat rides. He kept walking, finding not only new places but new streets, paved streets and cobblestone streets and a stretch of whitewashed wooden planks that simply came to an end in a hedge of skip laurels that bordered the college. He went as far as he could along the boardwalk and stood there for a time, staring into the shadows of the hedge, puzzled. Far off he heard the crying of shorebirds.

The next day his wife woke up agitated. She hadn't even started packing, she said. She asked him to get the hard-shell silver suitcase down from the attic. When he froze and said nothing, she said, Oh. Maybe a dream, he said. But there was no silver suitcase he could remember, and they didn't have an attic.

He found on his walk that the new eight-story building on Main was finished. Even so, one of the orange-vested construction workers was posting a new building permit outside the restaurant with the yellow and white striped awning.

What's happening, the man asked, stopping.

Need this space, said the construction worker.

For what? asked the man.

The worker checked his clipboard and said, A museum of blown glass, and the history and technology thereof.

Why? the man asked.

The worker shrugged. What's wrong with a museum of blown glass, and the history and technology thereof?

The man looked back toward the restaurant with the awning. I never even had a meal there, he said.

It wasn't bad, the worker said. But I'm excited about the museum.

When he went home, he found that they had a new picket fence around the yard, still wet with paint. And on the side of the house there was a garden, now, filled with strawberry plants and dotted with pinwheels that caught the morning sunlight.

We should talk, the nurse said, when he went inside. Things, she said, are moving quickly now.

He looked toward the closed door of the bedroom. Okay, he said.

She told him, again, what to expect.

Don't be surprised, she said. Things will get weird.

Things already, he said, seem weird.

He was thinking about his feet, which were now too small for his shoes. He'd had to hunt through the closet that morning to find an old pair of his wife's running shoes. Maybe, he thought, he should mention that to the nurse. But then she'd ask him if he'd rather his feet became larger, and he'd ask if they *had* to become one or the other, and she'd say Yes, it seemed that way.

His wife slept much of the day. She didn't want to be moved from the bedroom so he sat in the chair across from the bed. When she was asleep he opened the blue notebook and read through the notes and the lists. Favorite words (number one for her was *refrain,* because it meant both to stop and to keep going, while for him it was *endless,* regretted as soon as he said it aloud); least favorite holidays (Flag Day for both of them); catalogues of childhood friends, opening lines from books, the evolution of her movie candy preferences. Sometimes he added a star here or there, or a sunburst, or a heart. Sometimes he only sat and watched her sleep. Sometimes he slept too.

Once, they both woke up at the same time. The room was dark except for the light of the muted television on the dresser, which was showing an old episode of *Hawaii Five-O.*

Did you used to live in a house—he said, leaning forward in the chair, his voice hushed—with a low white picket fence? And a strawberry garden?

In the flickering TV light he could see her cloudy eyes go inward for a second: seeking, then finding. She nodded.

Sometime around dawn he woke up, still clothed and curled in the chair. The bed was empty. The room was different. Smaller than he remembered, with a full-sized bed instead of their queen, and butterfly wallpaper, and in the corner was an adolescent's white desk with an oval mirror, the kind with two faces, one that showed you up close and one that showed you as you were to everyone else. Branches scraped against the window, from a dogwood tree that had sprouted and matured overnight outside their bedroom.

He went to the door, and felt, behind him, the room already changing, moving on. The hallway was crowded with people coming and going, so much so that he had to move to the side to let them pass. Adolescent girls and crying teenagers, older adults who all looked a little like his wife, nervous boys and other boys who didn't look quite nervous enough, college girls in their bathrobes chatting on the way to the shower. They ignored him but he felt the rush of life as they moved past, like blood through an artery.

Things were moving so quickly now.

The streetlamps were still lit when he stepped out the front door and went down the steps. Autumn was here and it was cool enough, in the shadows of the skyscrapers that had gone up in the night, that he could've used a jacket. Goosebumps rose on his smooth skin. He walked to keep warm, thinking as he walked that he'd been trying to remember something, and that it was close, whatever it had been, and wasn't that the strangest feeling, to know that something was so deliciously close, to know that it was there but might never be found?

West End down to Eighty-Seventh, then east, toward the park. Shivering pleasantly.

Oh: the city waking up, all around, all around. A line at Eddy's already. The new Italian guy behind the counter, only his first week. Nervous, not great with his English, but friendly. Earnest. A little too earnest, but he'd figure it out. (So would she.) Then it was her turn to order, and she went to the counter and she saw his nametag, and she laughed.

Giuseppe, she said.

He smiled shyly and he didn't understand, but he laughed, too.

She took her coffee and sipped it as she crossed Columbus Avenue, then made her way into the park. She found a bench that looked out on the south side of the park, toward Midtown, and took small bites from her bagel. Across the way, a girl walked a path into the park with her mother, holding a bag of cotton candy in her hand, though it was still early in the morning. The city loomed high above the tree line, and she knew no one here, and there was time.

Babel

SUNDAY MORNING Petra wakes up to find her nail polish laid out on the bathroom counter, while her eleven-year-old son sits bent over in concentration on the tile floor. Eight of his toenails are purple.

"Was bored," says Del, without looking up.

"Okay, yeah. It's not even seven o'clock." Leans down for a closer look, says, "But you did an amazing job," which is true. On his toenails, anyway. The countertop and the floor have sustained some damage.

He stares down at his toes. Grimly serious.

Squatting down to inspect the bottle, Petra says, "Purple Mountains Majesty, a classic."

"I'm calling it something else." Squinting up at her now. "Can I do that?"

"Sure." When he was younger and still learning to read, Del liked to puzzle out the names, which led to an appreciation for puns that his teachers didn't share. "Something funny?"

"Apoopalypse."

"Always the poop jokes."

Shrugging, "Can I do my fingers too?"

She barely hesitates. "Go for it," she says. "A little less on the floor, though."

Petra spends the rest of the morning cleaning out the basement storage room and going through Del's winter clothes, trying to figure out what still fits and what she'll need to replace. He has stuff over at Mike's, but she's already heard the lecture about No Sharing Between Houses. Because That's How Things Get Lost, and by Things we mean things that Mike and Noreen bought. So, okay guys. Two pairs of galoshes it is.

Now and then Del asks her opinion about a new color. By late afternoon he's settled on a light blue shade that Petra can't remember buying.

"Blue Skies Ahead," she says.

"Morris the Orangutan," he counters.

"Okay, yeah."

She has to help him with the right hand, trying to draw him out without giving him the full-court press. Not easy with Del, whose first complete sentence came at age four. A lot of speculation about autism and other developmental disorders. The diagnosis changed every year, but to Petra, her son only seemed wrapped in this odd cloud of melancholy from which he periodically, though infrequently, emerged.

Cleaning up after dinner, she reminds him to take off the nail polish and tells him where he can find the remover.

"But why?" he asks.

"Well," she says, "school tomorrow."

"So?"

She hesitates. Sometimes she wonders if she isn't flawed in some fundamental way, lacking this parental instinct that everyone else is born with or magically acquires upon becoming a parent, the one that lets you automatically answer your kids with absolute conviction, immune from self-doubt. Instead, she usually—now being included—finds herself wondering if she's really qualified to dispense wisdom at all, even to an eleven-year-old. Especially to an eleven-year-old.

"Kids can be mean," she says. "You know how it is."

He turns his hands over and considers them for a long couple of seconds. "So you think I should take it off?"

Has to put her on the spot and call her out. So, what to say?

Well okay, yeah. Yeah, I think you should take it off. Because we live in a town where everyone is only who they're supposed to be and never anything else, and you'll get teased, and it's something the other kids will remember: that you're the boy who wore blue nail polish to school. You'll be *that* kid. And even though it shouldn't matter, it will. Long after you think it's forgotten, after you've discarded nail polish and moved on to the next curiosity of childhood—sizing yourself up, asking yourself who you are, what you're supposed to make of yourself—someone will be there to remind you that you were, what, a deviant? An eleven-year-old deviant, sure. And you don't even care about this stuff, any of it, but you will someday. Skip the nail polish and follow along like everyone else, toe the line, and sooner or later you'll be called out for something anyway, some little thing you never knew was wrong with yourself. The way you say your Rs, your taste in cartoons, the kind of clothes you wear or the way you wear them, the shape of your eyes, the way you pull at your lip when you're lost in thought. Your laugh, Jesus, your batshit crazy laugh. Someone will call you out, maybe not say anything but just give you a look, a smirk. A goddamn smirk. And then you'll care. You, Del, who have innocently and terribly never cared at all, will suddenly care. Because you won't want to be left out, you won't want to be the outcast, the dork, *that* kid, the one who just doesn't get it. And then, damn it all, kid, you'll do it to someone else. You'll take that from someone else, you'll take it with a shrug or a wisecrack to impress your friends, not even being mean, just trying to fit in. Because you'll forget this shit ever mattered, like everyone forgets it ever mattered. And maybe it doesn't anyway. Fuck, Petra. Maybe there's a remedial parenting course you can take online somewhere?

Del's still looking at her. Patient. Trusting that she'll give him good advice, because she's a parent and there's this whole infallible parental instinct thing.

"Sure, hey," she says, "leave it on. If the kids say anything, fuck 'em. Right?"

Which prompts a raised eyebrow, at least. And then he's off to play, the matter quickly and easily forgotten.

In the morning she drops Del off at Mike's before school. Still a little contentious, these Monday morning transitions. Letting Petra extend the definition of *weekend* to include a few extra hours with Del had been a moment of weakness for Mike at the time of the court hearing, and at least once a month Noreen suggests with her bug-eyed smile that they might want to revisit the agreement.

She carries his overnight bag in behind Del, gives him a hug while Noreen hovers, monster-like, in the background. He acknowledges Noreen with a grave little nod and then tears off to get his books for school.

"Really, Petra," Noreen says.

"Hmm," blinking at this.

"The nails." With a quick glance back toward the stairs, "You could've discussed it with us. We've all got to work together as a team, Petra, don't we?"

"Guess it didn't seem like it required a conference, Noreen?"

"But that's just it, isn't it? You guessing, I mean." With a thousand-watt smile, wholly unnatural.

"Not totally following," says Petra.

"The thing is," standing up and brushing off her pantsuit, symbolically Petra assumes, "*we* see Del all week long. So we have maybe a better sense of what Del needs, at this point? Than you? And we're the ones who have to deal with the consequences. I'm sure you can appreciate that, Petra, right?"

Mike has appeared in the middle of all of this, keys in his hand. Takes in the scene without saying a word, glancing back and forth between the two women.

Petra resists the urge to back up a step. "I'm sure he'll be fine."

"It's just, Petra," with a sidelong glance at Mike, "that we don't want Del to get hurt again. And you don't have the greatest track record? When it comes to keeping Del out of, well, harm's way?"

"Hey," says Mike.

"Ah," says Petra, "right." Feeling a little wobbly.

Del at that moment comes racing down the stairs, and the scene comes to an abrupt conclusion. Moments later she's in her car, heart thumping madly, speeding off into the gray morning with Noreen's words ringing in her ears.

At work, Petra drinks too much coffee, rereads the same paragraph onscreen for hours at a time, practices her trashcan basketball alley-oop skills. She tries not to wonder how things are going for Del, tries not to imagine all the different scenarios in which he's humiliated or disappointed or disillusioned by his classmates. Instead tries to imagine one scenario—there has to be one—in which none of those things happens, and Petra doesn't have to accept that she sent her son off to deal with that bullshit. Irresponsible. Fuck, maybe old bug eyes is right.

At three o'clock she calls Mike's place, finds Brittany between text messages. Asks about Del and gets the usual.

"He doesn't seem, well, a little off?"

"More than regular off?" says Brittany.

"So," when Del gets on the phone, Petra trying to sound nonchalant. "School," just to clarify. "Anything interesting?"

"You mean the nails." She can hear him flipping the page of one of his comics.

"Sure," says Petra.

"I'm thinking," he says, "of maybe purple tomorrow."

It's days before she hears the whole story, and even then she only gets bits and pieces from her son. The rest is fragmented and apocryphal, like an origin story from one of Del's comics, overheard in office hallways and coffee shops and grocery stores, half of countless cellphone conversations, worried parents wondering—in between shuttling their kids to yoga lessons and violin practice and Chinese immersion programs—what the fuck, exactly, is happening here.

What's happening is that on the day Del goes to school wearing Morris the Orangutan on his fingers, a dozen other boys come home with their own nails painted. Fruitless and one-sided interrogations ensue over a dozen dinner tables. Conversational lead-ins range from *Explain yourself* to *Is there something you'd like to discuss* to *Dear god why are you punishing us?* The boys blink quietly and reach for the potatoes with their sweetly glittering fingers.

The number doubles, then triples, and by Thursday, half the sixth-grade male population is sporting painted nails. Star-spangled nails, day-glo-green nails, burgundy and orange nails, skull and crossbone nails, checkerboard nails, zebra stripe nails, paisley nails, tie-dyed nails, superhero logo nails, camouflage nails, nails decorated with letters and zodiac symbols and emoticons, some crudely painted but others suggesting the assistance of experienced sisters, cousins, classmates. A few take to wearing makeup on their faces too, applied in bold streaks like war paint, and when Brent Bowman—face invisible under alternating layers of red and gold color—is sent home for some unstated violation of school policy, painted faces start appearing in every classroom, gestures of solidarity toward a cause the boys are either unable or unwilling to identify.

Del is cheerfully oblivious to the weirdness. Petra only knows that the world, or at the least the world of eleven-year-old boys, has mysteriously passed on the chance to put her oddball son in his place.

We are concerned about some recent behavior patterns, the first but not the last of the emails to be sent out by the middle school principal. The specific behavior patterns of concern remaining unstated, the idea being, maybe, that we all know what's going on here. A little more ominously, *the origin of the disruptive behavior is unknown, but we are investigating.* The word *disruptive* appears at regular intervals throughout the email, plosive drumbeats of danger.

There's a proportional response from the other flank. The girls start wearing boys' clothes to school: oversized pants and mismatched shirts, bandanas and chains, pink skullcaps, football and baseball jerseys, madcap eyepatches, their brothers' basketball shoes, blazers and ties stolen from their fathers' closets. They take on the boys' speech patterns, communicating with monosyllables and grunting, walk around with their suddenly polish-free hands stuffed in their pockets, and shoot rubber bands across the classroom at each other and at unsuspecting teachers. They yawn openly in class and stop brushing their hair. They draw crude pictures of boobs and penises inside the stalls of the girls' restroom.

Carly, who started the same day as Petra and has a niece at the school, supplies this last bit of gossip in the break room. "They're saying it's like a cult. Nobody's heard of such a thing."

"Who's saying?" Petra asks.

Shrugging, "Anyway my sister's bringing Jane to the doctor. Psychiatrist, psychologist, whatever."

"Maybe a little," says Petra, "extreme?"

"But these are like gateway behavioral patterns, is what they're saying."

Petra repeats the phrase, seeing it float in the air above her like a cartoon bubble.

"Del's good, though? No trouble?"

In fact, Del called Petra this morning while in the act of appropriating makeup from Noreen's bag while his stepmother slept, wanting to be done up like an Egyptian pharaoh.

Del, I'm not going to help you steal.

Well let's say I had permission. What would I need?

Later she received a text from Noreen—*maybe you can explain this*—along with incriminating photos. Del with thick gold and black mascara around the eyes, rope necklace, dangling hoop clip-on earrings he discovered in an old plastic bin in the basement. Also mismatched tennis shoes, green laces on the left, purple on the right. And a series of hieroglyphs penned along both forearms. Circle, crescent moon, squiggly thing like an ocean wave. Presumably important dots.

"No trouble at all," Petra tells Carly.

THE NEXT EMAIL from the principal arrives with the subject line, *On new policy re: gibberish in school.*

Whatever mutinous fever dream is overwhelming the student body has apparently spilled over into its language. Words are substituted randomly for other words, tenses added and subtracted, inflections changed and subverted. Boys and girls who are increasingly unrecognizable are now incomprehensible, too, at least to the parents and teachers who eavesdrop on their conversations. The kids themselves have either picked up the new language with maddening speed—chatting between classes, mock-fighting on the playground, passing exclamation-heavy notes in study hall—or else they're all complicit in some lunatic prank whose primary and only purpose seems to be frustrating anyone over the age of eleven.

It is imperative that we maintain order in our classrooms. So, for the duration of what the principal calls "the current crisis," Spanish and other non-English languages are to be classified as gibberish, the faculty being one hundred percent monolingual. The email closes with the announcement of an emergency meeting, and all *engaged, concerned parents* are invited to attend.

Petra hangs out in the back of the auditorium, invisible. Listens as teachers and then parents take the microphone. The whole thing takes on a weird post-traumatic stress support group vibe. Whitney's been dressing like a train hobo and hasn't turned on her phone in two days. Drew sits in bed at night reading the dictionary with a highlighter, giggling like a loon. Sarah's been giving away her toys, her clothing, her mom's jewelry to random girls she meets God knows where. Richie announced over dinner he's a pacifist—*and where'd he even learn that word?*—and won't be playing football or delivering the fist of justice to anyone this year. And more of the same. Their children, the children they knew, have been stolen from them.

The rhetoric intensifies and Petra feels herself start to detach. In Tbilisi, she heard her mother and grandfather arguing all the time. Petra's grandfather with his portrait of Stalin hanging in the living room, not so much a fan of mass murder as a loyalist to Georgia's most famous celebrity. Petra's mother, Irina, half his size, but making up for it with volume and arm waving. Arguments unintelligible to four-year-old Petra, who did her best to map the crossfired words against her limited vocabulary, seizing on the few familiar ones, like *dzaghli*, which she knew because of the hordes of stray dogs that plagued the city. Petra's grandfather and the other sanitation workers were charged with culling them. A task which, to his granddaughter's endless horror, involved snatching them up with massive iron claws that broke the dogs' backs. Petra was convinced the arguments were about the dogs, whose presence threatened, according to her grandfather, all of Georgia. Led by the mongrels Shanidze, Kostava, Gamasakhurdia, whom Petra imagined in great detail, prowling the highlands above the city in exile, noble even as they were hunted to extinction. She understood only that her mother, *moghalate*, was somehow in league with them, which fascinated her and gave her an appreciation for her mother that would last until they moved to America a few years later. Petra's too-eager assimilation into the American culture and language put an end to that.

In the school auditorium the talk turns to strategy, and when that doesn't prove fruitful, to assigning blame. *Someone started this. Things like this don't come out of nowhere.* Names are thrown around, families who aren't present and haven't, coincidentally, been totally and completely reliable. Getting too hot in the room. Petra slides out quietly, just as Brent Bowman's father, a police officer, floats the idea of bringing in a few of the kids for one-on-one interrogations. Just the known troublemakers. Just to get to the bottom of things.

Out in the street, Petra wanders.

Kids are everywhere. Some but not all of them dressed in rags or makeshift costumes, a few with painted faces. They're either communicating telepathically or talking just below eavesdropping level. Petra watches them move through the park and down past the skating rink alone and in pairs, in threes and fours and fives. Whenever two groups cross paths, some of the children in each group exchange places, like electrons gained or lost in some weird chemical reaction, cliques forming and dissolving, an infinite loop of rearrangement or reassignment or something else that Petra can't name. And all of it happening not quite in silence, but without any obvious direction from the children.

It's December and the sun falls early. The adults in town leave their offices and head out into the dusk, and the stream of children fades as they're called back home before the newly announced curfew. Petra's left with this melancholy vibe, brought on not so much by the presence of the adults around her—with their dark clothes and their secrets and their anxious, distracted faces—as by the children's absence, some gradual decline of energy.

On the way to her car, she runs into Mike.

"You left early," he said. Soft plumes of breath surrounded his face, still maddeningly youthful, like a halo.

She almost responds sharply but sees that there's no malice in the comment. "Suffocating in there, that's all."

"Yeah. Listen. Sorry about, you know, the other day. Stupid thing for her to say."

Petra shrugs, "I'm the fuck-up, Mike." Snow begins to fall. "A little too adorable a moment for me, hope you don't mind if I split?"

"As long as you know," he says.

"That you're sorry," she says. "Got it, Mike."

She drives a couple blocks in the snow and then pulls over. Opens the car door and surprises herself by throwing up. After sitting for a few minutes, she shuts off the ignition and gets out. Scoops up a handful of fresh snow to rinse her mouth, steadies herself against the car.

No, she doesn't want Del to get hurt again. To wander off while Petra fucks someone in an upstairs bedroom, drunk. Some nameless idiot she picked up because, well, because he looked tough and mean, he looked like he could beat Mike to a bloody pulp, which in those days seemed like an awfully good reason. Del, always the wanderer, half-present, long gone by the time she went in to check on him, still half-drunk. Then a bleak couple of hours, with a parade of flashlights bouncing through the woods as a light cold rain fell, self-hatred settling in for the duration. When Del was found, an hour before dawn, Petra caught her reflection in the window of the paramedics' truck. A madwoman wearing a robe made of dirt and leaves, her hair a shock of moonlight white, face empty. Sidelong glances, easily decoded, from the neighbors who had spent all night searching, who smelled the alcohol and the sex on her. *Not one of us.* Maybe she'd never been one of them. Never adjusted to the suburban life she'd accepted as part of the deal with Mike, and her disguise, like the false mask of a witch in a fairy tale, was finally wearing thin. Not a Georgian anymore either. Just a woman grown old, residing uneasily here, hopelessly liminal.

She leaves the car by the side of the road and walks. Not thinking about where she's going, she wanders over like some masochistic somnambulist to Hillwood Glen, the old neighborhood. Blandly imposing five-bedroom houses rise up along well-lit streets, each with a Wind or a Meadow or a Vale in its name. The holiday lights, already in place a week after Thanksgiving, seem perfectly coordinated from house to house, a coordination that Petra remembers to be anything but coincidental.

She'd preferred their apartment by the river and the train tracks. But the schools were better here, less crime, etc. And the house, the giant goddamn house with a three-car garage, because their two Mercedes needed room to breathe, possibly procreate. Petra's mother had come to visit exactly once, dismissing it all with a familiar and peculiarly Georgian shudder. The old radical, unrepentant and unchanged. She'd been arrested four times in Tbilisi and another four times in America, and she disapproved of Petra's clothes, house, husband, cars, all of it. Off somewhere now, either manning a picket line or working the front lines of the revolution, which these days means blogging mercilessly and, to Petra, incoherently. Their only conversation in the last five years was after the divorce, when Petra admittedly went off the rails a bit, the incident in the woods serving as only the final act of a pretty spectacular performance that, as a whole, gave Petra a brand-new reputation in town, and prompted the call from Irina. *You cracking up or waking up, bavshvi?*

Finding herself at the guardhouse, she taps on the glass.

"My lady Petra," with a bigger smile than she's encountered in a pretty long time, "didn't think it was pick-up time yet. Or are you just coming to see me?"

"Just being a vagrant tonight, Ray. How're the mean streets?"

"Manger pranks on the rise," says Ray, "'specially sheep theft. Plus someone thought it'd be funny to rearrange the street signs, so the folks on Rumbling Meadow are getting mail now for Rustling Heather Way. Tensions running high, as you'd expect."

"Crazy times," Petra agrees. "On my way. Say hi to Lula."

"Be good," Ray calls out as she departs, the words drifting past her like smoke rings. "Be safe. . . ."

Past Hillwood Glen, intermittently working streetlights announce the school district boundary. Children are out romping through the half-inch of snow, ignoring the curfew, some playing freeze tag and snake in the gutter, others just huddled together, heads curiously close, arms around shoulders. Even in the twilight Petra can see their mismatched clothes and painted faces and nails, streaks of color that, as the children move, carve through the dark like iridescent paint strokes on a black canvas. She walks on. Growing cold now, and her legs are stiffening. She passes other adults, their hands stuffed in winter coats and their eyes half-closed against the wind. There's a strange aimlessness to their movements. Petra wonders if they, like her, simply found themselves wandering for no good reason tonight. Searching or running. Petra isn't sure which of the two she's doing herself this evening, only that she has to keep moving.

Not far now from the river and her old pre-Del apartment with Mike. Only every fourth or fifth streetlight is working, casting yellow arcs of light on potholed streets that will only get worse as the winter progresses. She hears footsteps behind her, and turns. The footsteps stop immediately.

"Ah, fuck," she whispers, not trying to be paranoid here, but she gets moving anyway. Down side streets she once knew a lot better, past shuttered storefronts and thrift stores and tenements still on the far side of gentrification, her heels too loud on the cracked sidewalk. Music drifts down from an upper-story apartment, some Latin tune that lends the scene an unearned liveliness, masking the menace Petra suddenly feels or is imagining. Up ahead, a group of three or four shadows dislodge themselves from the wall and walk toward her. She turns and sees, or thinks she sees, others coming toward her in the gloom.

Someone grabs her hand. *Come*, and then she's being pulled inside the apartment building, down a half-lit hallway, around a corner, out the back exit and across the street and immediately into another building.

She allows herself to be led forward in the dark. Following behind her guide—a child, she thinks but can't be sure—she glides ghost-like past open doorways whose doors have long since been ripped off their hinges, through which she sees the shadowy forms of men, women, children. Huddled on old mattresses and under blankets, in candlelit rooms filled with cast-off furniture and stuffed animals the color of ash, refugees from some localized apocalypse that didn't make the evening news. A young girl looks up at Petra as she moves past. She's pulled forward by her guide, around hallway corners and deeper into the building. Deeper in, graffiti covers the walls, lit imperfectly by the refracted glow of streetlamps and passing headlights. Here are idealized women and sunglassed street toughs, anthropomorphic dollar signs, lines of scripture and hip-hop lyrics, a Last Supper of anime girls with Alice in Wonderland eyes, long-forgotten names emblazoned in five-foot neon letters. Here are declarations of revenge, love, remembrance, the words faded and painted over, letters repurposed for another message, so that the final "E" in ELVIS RULES becomes one of the "E"s in the stoner-cryptic WHOEVER YOU ARE, MAN. Farther along the images and text grow less distinct. Her eyes play tricks as she's pulled faster, toward some unimaginable terminus in the center of the building or maybe the center of the earth, and here, at the bottom of things, she begins to see, or thinks she begins to see, repeated and familiar shapes: circles, crescent moons, ocean waves. Barely visible beneath layers of graffiti, as if they've always been here, ancient and original. She calls out again, Wait, and the small hand in hers slips free. A young voice recedes in the dark: You'll be okay now, and then a door opens at the end of the hallway and December rushes back in.

It's late when she finally makes it back to her car, miraculously untowed. At home she sits in the bath and tries to come back to herself, but she's nowhere to be found.

Later, on the phone with Del, she says, "Do you ever go down by the river? To where we lived before you were born?"

"You sound weird," he says. "You okay?"

"I'm fine." She realizes she's drawing shapes on the kitchen counter, tracing them invisibly with her finger, and stops. "Del," she asks, "you weren't out tonight, were you?"

"Curfew," he says.

Which isn't quite an answer. Later, lying in bed trying to fall asleep, Petra stares up at the shadows on the ceiling. Imagines Del's hieroglyphs, recombining endlessly, spelling out something in a language she can almost, but not quite, understand.

~

Friday after work, Petra stops and grabs takeout on her way to get Del. Over naan and chicken tikka masala she learns that he's supposed to see a psychiatrist on Monday.

"At the school?" she asks.

Shaking his head, "Think it's Noreen's psychiatrist."

"You don't have to do that, Del."

"I know," very simply. Then: "Some kids got suspended for talking gibberish."

"Heard about that. So what's next?" As if she takes it for granted that there's a next, that this is all moving inexorably toward, well, something. Which is almost as ridiculous as thinking that Del will tell her what's on his mind.

"Something new," he says. "Silent."

"Sign language," Petra suggests, and then, holding up her hand, "I know, I wouldn't get it. Age restrictions and whatnot."

"I can show you." And he walks her through it. Not sign language or not exactly sign language. Not a true correspondence, but instead a set of ideas, coded into the tilt of the head, the sweep of an arm, the texture of a smile.

"What ideas," as she tears off a piece of bread. "Say something to me."

He holds open his hand, palm open and fingers splayed, and then in a slow quiet motion he curls the fingers around into a fist, which he lifts and then moves across his body as if he's tracing the arc of the moon. Then he pulls the fist toward his chest as he closes his eyes.

"What does it mean," Petra says.

"It's like," says Del, "when you're in a fight and you don't know what to say, how to end it. Or like, 'let's be good to each other.' Just that."

She shivers a little at this. "Why can't you just say that in English, though."

Shrugging: "I don't know."

"Tell me something else."

For the next half-hour he talks, he shows her his silent language, and she watches and listens. Sometimes she suggests things, asks questions, even makes up her own signs. Eventually they stop talking completely. They sit on either side of a table full of dirty dishes, barely moving at all, and they say these things to each other, among many other things:

I miss your laugh.

You look so lost sometimes.

You have beautiful teeth.

Sometimes I feel that I'm not good enough for you.

This moment, I am troubled.

Sometimes I am disappointed with the world.

There's nothing to be forgiven.

I am humbled, and shaken, by your love for me.

Let's be good to each other.

I am happy for this moment.

~

LATER THEY'RE on the sofa together under a blanket, head to toe, while an old Jimmy Stewart movie plays on television. Del's asleep, snoring gently beneath a bowl of popcorn. Petra's in the process of attempting to transfer the bowl of popcorn to the coffee table without waking Del when a brick comes through the window above the front door, and the popcorn goes flying. She's on her feet and tearing through the closet to find the baseball bat without any real awareness of what she's doing, moving soundlessly, or maybe it's only that there's a ringing in her ears and it's all she can hear. She only starts to become fully aware of herself minutes later, with her back to the wall beside the door, gripping the bat so tightly that her hand will be bruised for days.

Del stares down in fascination at Petra's bare, bloody feet.

ON SUNDAY the fires start to appear. In the parking lots of yoga studios and coffee shops, on construction sites in gated communities, in overflowing trashcans on neglected playgrounds. Never large enough to cause great damage, never endangering anyone. Almost—this is what Petra thinks—as if they're totems, fire spirits erupted from the earth or the heavens, hard to tell which. The running apocrypha is that all the fires go up at once. And so all through the day on Sunday, if you were to walk outside, you'd see dozens of columns of white smoke rising from the earth. You'd hear an unsettling silence punctuated only by the sound of the fire trucks moving from scene to scene. Giving the town the general character and appearance of either a war zone after all the combatants have been slain, or the breathless aftermath of an armistice.

Standing outside with Del, Petra sees her neighbor across the street staring back at them. Petra lifts her arm, opens her hand, palm forward. A sign. *I see you, and it's okay.* The blinds close, in a way you'd have to call pretty abruptly. Another sign.

THE TRANSITION is quiet, uneventful. Maybe too uneventful. Later Petra gets a call from Noreen and Mike, on speaker.

We think Del should stay with us for a while. Until all of this plays out.

The conversation lasts a while. When it's over, Petra walks to the closet, a little dazed, and takes out the baseball bat. Then she goes from window to window on the first floor of the house. When she's done, she carefully cleans up the glass. She curls up on the sofa as the curtains blow ferociously behind her. Her hands are balled into fists against her chest, and she thinks: how strange. They smell like gasoline.

~

"House arrest," Mike says, a couple days later. "Of course they're not calling it that. It's like suspension, except they've got like a car stationed outside and they told us not to let him leave. They think it's like an occult thing."

Del isn't the only one. Maybe two dozen other boys and a handful of girls, "the ringleaders," Mike says, which makes Petra laugh.

Turns out one of the boys on house arrest is Brent Bowman. One morning he's in with the private tutor, and his mom walks in and asks him, kind of absently, what's the name of that breakfast cereal you like, and Brent says well, okay, if I'm being totally honest then I'll say I'd rather have yogurt, and his mom shrieks because, upon closer inspection, the boy sitting at Brent's desk with the private tutor isn't Brent at all but some other kid. And isn't even, technically, a boy.

The scene plays out across town, as parents everywhere discover that their children have been interchanged, scattered haphazardly between houses like playing cards. The children jump out of bed, laughing, lacking even the good sense to be properly mortified by the shame of discovery. Instead they stare innocently at their adopted parents, asking to be seen, to be provided for. To be, of all things, loved.

Petra falls asleep and dreams of the dogs. She dreams it's her job to spot them and point them out to her grandfather, who's standing by with his iron claws. She understands that she can protect the dogs only by not seeing them. But she can't help it. She can't help betraying them, giving them away. Her grandfather pats her on the head and comforts her, and then he goes off to slaughter the dogs.

When the morning comes again, the children are gone.

Clothes are left in drawers, pajamas on the floor where they've fallen, textbooks neatly stacked on dressers. No notes are left behind.

With the rest of the town, Petra goes out to search. The fires are still burning and the town smells of smoke and ash. They head, all of them, to the highlands beyond the town's northern boundary. For no reason except that there's no other place to look. They make their way silently, through the tall grass, while behind them the fires smolder and the streets lay empty and quiet. They're anxious and uncertain. The children may, must surely be, there beyond the next rise. Or the one after that.

Petra looks back. A ghost town, behind her, purified by fire.

She looks ahead. No sign of anything, really, except the advancing night. Huddled forms with their faces to the ground, unsure where they are, what they're seeking, what they're prepared to find. She wants to reach out to them, to say something comforting, but they share no language for this.

Far away, Petra sees a familiar face. For a few moments they stare at each other across some implausible distance, the tall grasses swaying between them, too far from each other to make eye contact. Mike raises his hand in front of him, so that she can see his nails. Painted baby blue. He closes his fingers into his palm, making a fist. And then he raises his arm and moves his fist in a slow, sweeping arc across his body.

The Night Parade

DYLAN'S IN A MOOD when I pick him up. He submits dead-armed to the hug, and when I squeeze him for an extra second, he presses his mouth against my ear and whispers, "You smell like butts." Then he shrugs me off and climbs into the back seat of the car.

Harry meets me in the driveway to hand me Dylan's backpack. "Mitch," he says. Voice booming. He's a booming-voice kind of person.

"Harry," I say. "How's Trish?" I can see her at the living room window, watching us from behind the curtain.

"Frankly worried," says Harry. "Nauseated."

"Ah. Well."

"You know how she is. Anyway." He looks to the car before turning back to me. "How are we feeling about the weekend? Positive?"

This stings a little. The last time Dylan stayed with me was admittedly not great. I'd taken him to a ballgame, the Nats' weekend opener against his favorite team, the Cubs. Turned out the box seat tickets I'd ordered and printed online as a special treat were fake, which we discovered at the entrance gate. Dylan and I got into it then. The usual stuff. He said I probably knew from the beginning that the seats weren't any good and it was all a joke because I didn't even like the Cubs. I said of course I didn't like the Cubs because we lived right outside of Washington. I said the weird thing was that he *liked* the Cubs even though he'd never been to Chicago, and even though he knew his own father was a diehard Nats fan. He said only the stupidest people he knew were Nats fans, so I said then probably he should be a Nats fan too. He blinked and said, So you're calling your own son stupid, and I said, Why does the opinion of a stupid person matter to you anyway, and he said, If I had three wishes right now I'd use all three to wish you were dead. We both let that one sit there for a minute between us.

Then I said it sounded like he didn't even need a dad anymore, and he said he absolutely didn't need a dad, and he could prove it, because I wasn't any kind of a dad and he was still managing okay, plus Harry was more of a dad than I'd ever be. I suggested that maybe he could find his own way home then, since he was Mr. Ungrateful Independent Baby Boy, and he said, Are you really threatening to leave me alone in the city, and I said, Of course not, and he said, It sure sounds like you are and only a horrible father would suggest that, and I said, Well only a miserable son would say the things you said about Harry being more of a dad than I'll ever be, and that was when he ran off into traffic and disappeared. The police found him three hours later trying to hitch a ride home.

So the question stings. But I don't hold it against Harry. I try not to hold it against Harry. Since the divorce he's always provided for Dylan and Trish. Provided too much, maybe? No. No one could ever say that, even if sometimes it can seem like too much, to some, just at times. But even so. Hard to begrudge them anything. Plus, I've been seeing a therapist. Court mandated! But still. I'm learning strategies. For example I'm supposed to go through a list of prime numbers in my head whenever I start to get upset or feel like things are spiraling out of control.

"Ha ha," I say. "Feeling extra positive in fact."

"I don't know if that's a thing, Mitch."

"Well," I say.

"Anyway, go easy on the little guy," he says. "He was invited to a friend's party at the lake this weekend. So he's, you know."

"The lake."

"Tahoe," says Harry. "The other kid's dad was going to fly them out in his private jet—*is* going to fly the others out now, I mean. But it was a last-minute thing. You know how it is. Dylan gets it." He smiles and nods at Dylan, sitting in the car. It's a very toothy smile. Sometimes I think that he, Harry, has too many teeth. Not in a bad way, just in a weird way. Or that they're too visible, or too white, or something. It's actually kind of sad. It actually makes you think he probably gets weird looks all the time because of his extra, highly visible super-white teeth.

I tell him I have something planned too, something kind of big. Which is true.

The smile dims as he looks back at me. Just a bit. Like a baby cloud has settled over Harry's smile. Is it possible he's worried? Maybe wondering if Dylan might come back Sunday raving about the old man, for once? Ha ha.

"Great to hear," he says. "Really. That'll make Dylan happy, that you've gone to the trouble of planning something. He'll appreciate that."

I don't know how to answer. So I only smile for a few seconds until my face begins to hurt. (Two, three, five. Is seven a prime? Maybe seven.) I look again toward the living room window, just in time to see Trish disappear behind the curtain.

~

"Are we even doing anything?" Dylan asks. "Like this whole weekend. Are we doing anything?"

We're back at the apartment. Dylan's already hooked up the game console he brought from his mother's house. He's wearing VR gloves and boots. One hand holds a Coke while he waves the other around as if he's conducting an orchestra. I can picture him suddenly as a grown-up: my son the famed orchestra conductor. Sponsored by Coke maybe?

"Loads of things," I tell him. And I leave to grab the Weekend Agenda binder from the kitchen counter.

"I'm not doing anything lame," Dylan calls out.

Friday is on top. I read it over silently.

4 p.m. - 6 p.m.
Unwind and Casual Conversation

6 p.m. - 7 p.m.
"Dylan Memories" Bingo!

7 p.m. - 8 p.m.
Surprise Dinner (Hint: Pizza!)

8 p.m. - 10:30 p.m.
Movies "on the green" ha ha

10:30 p.m. - ???
The Perseids

"Like I'm not going to just sit around *talking*," Dylan says, eyes on the TV. I watch as he stomps something violently with his VR boot. I can't quite tell what it is. But a burst of yellow and green viscera explodes out of the body, so I'm thinking it isn't human.

"Well I mean the schedule's flexible." Wondering if I should move Bingo up one slot. I ordered special Bingo cards and matching Bingo balls with memorable and funny phrases from Dylan's childhood. For example: "Pasta!" Also for example: "Where's my boogie?!" Some are just photos of Dylan, or Dylan and me, like from the trip we took to Niagara Falls together right after the divorce. We were on the Maid of the Mist boat tour and Dylan had an anxiety attack and vomited all over himself, others, because it turned out he had a fear of boats and a fear of water and a fear of waterfalls especially. But the picture was from before he threw up, and it's just the two of us standing on the deck in blue raincoats, with his little hand in mine. He looks so trusting. So unaware of the coming vomit storm. Anyway there are like thirty different "memories" like that. Plus I bought a bingo machine, one of those cages with a hand crank. Originally I'd found a build-your-own version I was going to order, and I was going to use the 4 p.m. - 6 p.m. slot for us to assemble it together. I thought that would make the actual bingo even more special. But the last time we tried to build something together, a go-kart from a kit I bought online for Dylan's sixth birthday, I tripped over an extension cord and hit my head on the edge of the coffee table, and by the time the paramedics left at midnight, Dylan had locked himself in the bathroom and wouldn't come out until the morning.

"And like if it's a game," he says, "I will literally barf."

"Well," I say. "I mean you're playing a game now."

"This is Justice Force VII. It's literally the greatest game ever invented."

For a few minutes I watch him play. "So there," I say. "I mean, it looks like you set fire to that orphanage."

"And?" he says.

"And then, like, ran away."

"And?" he says again.

"Just seems, I don't know."

He pauses the game so he can do something with his phone. When he's done, he sets the phone back down and resumes playing.

My phone buzzes a second later. I see a notification from Blabbr that Dylan has just posted. I tap to open the app. The post is just an emoji of a screaming head holding a gun to itself.

I cross Bingo off the list.

We end up ordering pizza early, then making sundaes and watching a movie. The plan is to watch "on the green," which means out in the common area of the apartment complex, with a new projector and movie screen I'd ordered, but when we go out to set things up we find another family already there, with an even bigger screen, plus bean bag chairs and a concession stand and a labradoodle wearing a little hat that says TICKET TAKER. I can see Dylan is a little disappointed. We carry everything back up and I get the screen set up in the living room in front of the actual television, which isn't perfect, but his face lights up when he sees I've rented his favorite movie: *Psycho Hell Clown 2: Splatterday Night Special.* Unfortunately we only have the theatrical version, not the uncensored director's cut, which Dylan says includes crew-shot footage of an accidental dismemberment on set. Halfway through the movie, Dylan's friends text him a photo from Lake Tahoe, where they've just run into the actor who plays Hell Clown.

"It's like I'm being literally tortured," he says, not looking at me.

"It's such a weird coincidence though," I say. "I mean, isn't it?" On screen, Hell Clown is holding a live poodle over his gaping jaw.

Dylan doesn't answer. Instead he furiously posts again on Blabbr. I get the notification but ignore it. Instead, I check the weather for the twentieth time. Happy to see the skies are clear.

Once the credits roll, I check my watch. It's not yet nine, and just getting dark outside. But Dylan is restless. So I stand and ask him if he's ready for the main event.

He eyes me suspiciously but sets his phone down. "You got Parade tickets?" He's been asking to go to the Night Parade for six months, since the Executive Order was passed.

"Not exactly," I say.

"Right. Of course." He lifts his phone and taps the Blabbr icon.

"It's something you've never seen before," I tell him. "That's all I want to say just yet. Maybe just trust me, this once?"

He turns his head back to me, and in his clouded young face I see all the things he might say in response to that. All the ways I've disappointed him. He looks like he's turning it over in his mind, considering whether to say something terrible. "You promise I'll like it?" he asks.

I swallow. And then I promise.

"All right," he says.

~

A HALF HOUR later we're at the Dawes Hill Wildlife Preserve parking lot. Dylan's face is pinched but he says nothing.

I tell him to help me unload as I pop the trunk. He blinks at what I've packed: cooler, blanket roll, two lawn chairs, two Coleman lanterns, and a grocery bag full of snacks.

"We're going camping," he says, defeated.

Instead of answering, I light both lanterns. Setting one down behind the car, I slide my arm through the handle of the other, tuck the blanket roll under my armpit, and grab the cooler and the grocery bag with my free hand. I can feel Dylan's eyes on me as I head toward the trailhead, but he says nothing. A few seconds later I hear the trunk close, and when I look back, he's close behind with the two chairs, the second lantern aglow in front of him.

We make our way silently as the night darkens. The trail isn't well marked and the trees block most of the light from the moonless sky. But I remember the way. It's been almost thirty years, but I remember.

Eventually we come to a wide, flat clearing. It's not the highest point at Dawes Hill, but it's the place with the clearest view of the sky, at the edge of the park alongside one of the older residential neighborhoods in town. I pick a soft, grassy spot in the middle of the clearing to set everything down.

Dylan scans the area, then checks his phone. "There no signal here," he says.

I tell him not to worry and point to the sky. "The show's up there," I say.

He tilts his head up. "Fighter jet flyover," he guesses. "I've seen them."

I tell him this is better.

He rolls his eyes but his face is still open, still trusting. Maybe not as trusting as he looked on the Maid of the Mist, pre-vomit, but still moderately trusting. He helps me lay the blanket and set up our spread. Chips, peanuts, pretzels, plus these chocolate caramel snacks that Dylan had on a trip to England with his mom and Harry, which I special-ordered. The last thing is a six-pack of beer. I pop one of the tops and hand it to Dylan, who raises an eyebrow but accepts it wordlessly.

I tell him the story, or at least some of the story, about coming here with my father. I was a year younger than Dylan, and like most boys that age, I worshipped my father. Of course I was terrified of him too, but that was mostly because he worked as a butcher, so he was always covered in blood when he came home. Hug him, my mother would say. Hug your father! And I'd stand halfway down the stairs, paralyzed with fear and horror, again as boys often are around their fathers. It's just pig and cow blood, she'd say. The boy doesn't need to hug me, my father would say. He does, she'd say. He's afraid and he doesn't, my father would say. Then he's no son of mine, she'd say, and he'd say, Just let it be, Margie, and she'd say, Don't undermine me, goddamn it, and he'd say, I work all day and I'll undermine if I want to. And she'd say, Great, why not, because everything else is going to hell in this house, and he'd say, Why do you have to be so damned dramatic? And she'd say, Oh, right, I forgot, we can only have one drama queen in the family, Mr. Cries in His Sleep, and then he'd throw down his bloody apron and storm upstairs to take a shower and splash mint-scented aftershave all over himself.

I don't tell Dylan all that. I only tell him about the night I came with my father to Dawes Hill, when we brought lawn chairs and sat in the same spot we're sitting in now. My father didn't drink much but he'd brought along a six-pack, and he let me have one. We didn't have much to say, really. We'd never spent much time together and didn't know each other well, and he was a quiet person anyway. But I was happy to be there with him, even if he hadn't told me the reason. I was especially happy because he hadn't gone to work that day and didn't smell so much like blood. He smelled like mint, or at least minty blood, which was better. We sipped our beers, and then at around ten o'clock my father jumped from the chair and turned to face me. It was dark and I could only see his eyes, bright and a little wild.

"What'd he say?" Dylan asks. "What'd he do?"

"He waved his arm—like this." I sweep my arm across the night sky. "Like he was opening a show before a crowd. And he laughed, and then he bellowed"—here I lift my head so I can do my best impression of Rod Steadman, age fifty-seven, bringing the thunder and the lightning one night in 1983— *"Let there be light!"*

Dylan laughs, and so do I. I laughed at the time too, because it was crazy, and so out of character for my father. In the very next moment I saw the first meteor streaking across the black sky. As if my father, a quiet butcher from New Jersey, had summoned it himself.

"The Perseids." I smile at Dylan. "I didn't even know they were coming, but he did. The biggest meteor shower of the year. And that night there was no moon, and it was the peak. Just like tonight. . . ."

We both look up. Overhead, the skies remain dark.

"Maybe it's still too early," Dylan suggests. "But we can just sit and watch. Right?"

We lie on the grass and fold our hands behind our heads and watch. Every few minutes we think we see something—*there, there, no there, where I'm pointing*—but mostly we're quiet. I can feel anxiety bubbling up because the meteors aren't coming the way I hoped, the way I remembered as a boy, watching with my father: one after the other, and then in pairs and triplets, screaming across the black heavens in a way that made me want to sob without knowing why. Because I was overcome with something. Maybe just with the feeling of being overcome. And when I looked at my father I could see in his face that he felt it too, and I loved him for that.

"I don't know what's happening," I say, pushing myself up on my elbows.

"You don't have to freak out," says Dylan.

(Five. Seven. Eleven.) "I'm not *freaking out*. It's just that we should've seen some by now."

"You're sure it's, like, the right date."

I clench my jaw. (Thirteen.)

"Well," Dylan says, "I kind of like it anyway. It's peaceful."

"Fuck peaceful." I take a breath. "I just mean that this isn't it. It's so much better. It *should be* so much better." I look toward the tree line to the north, wondering if they're lower on the horizon this year somehow.

Dylan rises beside me. "Dad," he says. "There!"

Then he's on his feet, and I'm on my feet too, and there—*Zing!* A shooting star from the northeast, careening silently past. It's followed by not only one but four others—*Zing! Zing! Zing! Zing!* Streaking right to left across the sky and leaving ghost trails behind. The last one glows like a struck match before expanding into a white and green fireball as it soars past.

Dylan gasps, and his face lights up as if he's five years old again on Christmas morning. For a few endless minutes we're silent, both of us just taking it in. The meteors come alone and in bursts of three, four, five, crisscrossing and in parallel, flaring brightly or fading softly, and it's exactly what I was hoping it would be. Dylan laughs as if he can't help himself, the way I laughed with my father all those years ago, the way my father laughed, at the sheer delight of it. Now this—I think—this is a night parade! Which is actually kind of a perfect thought. A night parade! I wonder if I should repeat that for Dylan. Better, obviously, if I'd just said it off the cuff, so it would sound like just some bit of casual brilliance from the old man. Not that it *won't* be off the cuff if I repeat it out loud. It would just be slightly less off the cuff. I should just repeat it. Without making a big deal out of it, but also *kind* of making a big deal out of it, in a natural and subtle and wisely paternal sort of way. Because it's important to get the tone right with some things, when they're things you'll remember forever. Neil Armstrong didn't step onto the surface of the moon and just blurt something out. He was *measured.* He understood the gravity of it all. The gravity! Wow. I'm sort of on fire now, and I'm overflowing with confidence as I lean toward Dylan and say softly, yet nonchalantly, yet reverently, "Now *this*, my son, is a—"

In that moment a bank of floodlights comes on, and the field is bathed in artificial light. The night sky disappears.

"What," says Dylan, "the actual fuck."

"This can't be happening." I squint toward the lights, which are mounted on poles positioned along the perimeter of the park. They look like stadium lights, half-hidden by the trees, but it makes no sense because the clearing isn't a ballfield, and there's no sane reason to put lights up here. I walk toward them, and as I get closer, I see the poles are mounted outside the park fence. They're in someone's back yard.

"Just a misunderstanding," I say, turning back to Dylan as I continue walking. "We'll just go talk to them."

"I feel like everything's ruined now," he says, following me.

"It's not *ruined*." (Twenty-three! Maybe!)

Now I can make out two figures as they step forward from the shadows, stopping twenty feet behind the fence to watch Dylan and me approach. One leans on a cane. The other, shorter and wearing a baseball cap, looks to be a skinny boy around Dylan's age.

"Excuse me!" I call out as I reach the fence. "The lights! Can you! Please! Shut the lights off!" Yelling but also smiling, to show that I'm polite and mostly harmless, but maybe not completely harmless. A person to be taken seriously.

The two figures turn to each other and confer. The shorter one takes a few steps closer, and I see now that it's a girl, not a boy. She's Chinese, maybe, and a black ponytail swings beneath the baseball cap as she moves. Her fingernails are painted glow-in-the-dark blue. "My father says no," she calls down.

"Well," I say, with my biggest smile, "he can't just say no, can he?"

"Dad," says Dylan, coming up behind me.

"He says no," the girl repeats. "He says—" She stops and looks back up at her father, who says something to her in another language. Probably

Chinese. She turns back to us and explains: "He says people come here and steal his chickens. He says it's not right. He says he has to protect us."

"Chickens!" I laugh out loud. I tell her we're not here to steal any chickens, we're just here to watch the once-in-a-lifetime meteor shower, which they would no doubt enjoy too if her father would simply turn off the—

"He says no. He says he doesn't want any trouble and you should go." She turns away again and starts back up toward the house.

"This blows," says Dylan.

I grab the fence and shake it, furious now. These people! Who are clearly not from around here! (Eleven! Seventeen! Twenty-something!) Ruining what was about to become one of the most important and formative experiences of my son's life!

"You don't want trouble? Really? Really?" My voice is rising and I know I'm supposed to keep cool in front of Dylan. But. Well, couldn't it be a good thing for him to see how his old man can fight for what's right? Would Harry run away with his tail between his legs in this situation? Of course not. Not Harry, with his five hundred gleaming white stupid teeth and his money and his glorious way of just knowing how to "do" things all the time.

I start climbing the fence.

"Dad. Holy shit," says Dylan.

"You've got trouble now!" I shout. "Trouble is exactly"—breathing a little hard, but still climbing—"what—you've—got!"

The girl with the black ponytail under the baseball cap approaches the fence and watches me, head slightly cocked. It's harder than I remember to climb a fence, but I've still got it. I'm not going to be stopped.

"You should go now," says the girl.

I reach the top, gasping. "You're going to call the police, I guess?" I scoff, or try to scoff, but I'm out of breath and I end up in a coughing fit instead. When I'm done coughing, I say, chillingly I hope, "Somehow I doubt that."

"Maybe you need to go back to China," Dylan says, below me.

"We're from Malaysia."

"Then why were you speaking Chinese?" I say.

Dylan barks a laugh. "Good one, Dad."

The girl sighs and walks to a wooden post near the chicken coop, then opens the door to a silver control box. "I am sorry," she says.

"You'll *be* sorry," says Dylan.

There's a crackle of electricity and *pop!* the fence comes to life beneath me, and my body somersaults backward through the air and onto the ground. I land on my back with my head thudding against the dewy grass, and everything goes black.

When I come to, I'm looking up at Dylan, whose face is framed, sort of angelically, by the floodlights.

"That was lit," he says. "I'm not even gonna lie."

He helps me to my feet. My back is screaming and my hands are a little burned from where I'd been gripping the fence. The father and daughter have disappeared back inside the house. As we pack up our things, Dylan asks if they're even allowed to be there. I tell him I don't know. He says it really stinks and I tell him I agree. We're both quiet as we walk back to the car and start home.

"We still had some fun though," I say. "Right? Still pretty unforgettable, I mean. At least *I* think."

Dylan grunts at this, head down in his phone again.

We come to a traffic light and coast to a stop. There's a billboard on the far corner that looks like a billowing American flag, except that it's tinted red because of the traffic light. Along the bottom is the regular message. *If you see something, say something.*

"We'll do something fun tomorrow," I promise.

"Whatever."

I ask him what that means.

"Nothing." *Ding.* Another Blabbr post is launched into the wild. A post no doubt about the old man. My stomach twists into a knot. (Thirty-one! Thirty-seven!)

"I tried my best tonight," I tell him. "I hope you realize that."

He shrugs. "That's what's sad about it." *Ding.*

I wait for the light to change, stewing quietly. "So you think, what. That I'm just going to let them get away with what they did tonight?"

He's interested again. "You mean we can get even somehow?"

My eyes fall on the flag billboard. "We could do something. Say something."

Dylan considers this. "What'll happen to them?"

"They'll get rattled a little. Agents at their door. Scare them a bit."

"Nothing more?"

"Not unless they've done something."

"They deserve it," he says. "*We're not Chinese.*" He says this with what I think he believes is a Chinese accent.

"I mean it's not about *that*, exactly." It feels like maybe we should discuss this. But it also feels like we're bonding again.

He taps his phone for a few seconds. "I've got the address." With a big smile on his face now. Seeing that smile just brings me joy. And it makes me realize a few things. How much I love seeing my boy happy, for one. What father doesn't live for a son's happiness? But also: I realize that the big gestures are overrated. It's all about connecting, that's all. Sometimes that means standing together under a field of shooting stars, but maybe, sometimes, it also means sending an anonymous text together to put a scare into an awful Malaysian family.

"What do I say?" he asks. "That they're terrorists?"

"We can't say that."

"Why not?"

We agree to say that we can't say they're *not* terrorists. That if we heard these particular people were terrorists, we wouldn't be exactly surprised. Because of certain things we've seen. Certain not quite American things. Lights coming on late at night, etc.

"What's the et cetera?" Dylan asks.

I tell him it means there are also zero or more additional suspicious things beyond the lights coming on late at night, and he says, "Nice, Dad."

He reads the text back to me. It's pretty well-balanced. I mean, it's not as if it's true, what we're saying. But it's not as if it's not true, either. We can't know. That's the thing. We can't know if they're insurrectionists working to secretly undermine our way of life, or if they're insurrectionists who could just someday in the future work to secretly undermine our way of life. And anyway it doesn't matter. If they've done nothing wrong, it'll all get cleared up and everyone will know they're innocent of any wrongdoing. Sort of a win-win, when you think about it.

"Sent," he says. "Too cool. Thanks, Dad. Sorry about the other stuff."

I'm practically beaming the rest of the way home.

THE NEXT MORNING I decide to call in a favor with my friend Tony.

"Kid's a minor," he says. "It'll be on me if he gets caught." Tony runs the local security operation for the monthly Night Parade weekend in our county. We've done weekend metal detecting at the Civil War battlefields, and Tony's a good guy. Is he a good guy with maybe an opioid addiction, who has made some suspect decisions to support that addiction? Maybe. But that's between Tony and God. And I guess me.

I tell him we absolutely won't get caught. "We get masks to wear, right? Nobody will know."

"This is it," he says. "Then we're even."

"But still buddies," I say.

"Asshole," he says.

It's all I can do not to tell Dylan and spoil the surprise. I'm not even bothered when he walks out in the middle of Dylan Memories Bingo to stand outside on the balcony and scream, then posts on Blabbr that he's descended into the tenth circle of Hell. Instead I respond to the post with a crazy-eyes emoji and write, *But you are loved so it can't be Hell!*

"Why are you acting so weird?" Dylan asks after dinner. He's playing Justice Force VII again, and I'm sitting on the couch, watching and smiling. And flinching sometimes. On the screen, he's corralling a dozen tentacled monsters into a pen, jabbing them with some kind of electric prod that makes them scream and twitch horribly.

"I'm just expectant," I tell him.

"Like you're having a baby?" he says. "Gross."

"Ha ha," I say. "Let's just say I think tonight's going to beat last night's show."

"It'll beat you getting electrocuted by a little Chinese girl?"

"She was Malaysian."

"Who cares?" he asks.

"Whatever," I say. "The point is that it's better."

"Stop being a dork and just tell me."

"One of your monsters is escaping," I tell him.

"Dang it." Instead of going after it, he snaps his fingers to change the electric prod into a blaster, and fires on the remaining monsters in the pen. They explode like propane tanks, sending multicolored brains and flesh everywhere. Then he hits the reset button and starts over. "That was your fault," he says.

"It's the Night Parade," I say.

He pauses the game, and turns to face me. "You mean it?"

"I mean it."

His face lights up slowly, a sunburst over his sweet features. Seeing it makes me realize that, actually, the little things might be great, but sometimes you do need the big things, too. Just to show you love them. More than other people love them? Ha ha, no. But yes, maybe.

~

DOWNTOWN THERE'S an electricity in the air like I've never felt before. It's magical.

We both feel it, as soon as we get through security and collect our complimentary masks and swag bags. The shops around the town square, where the parade comes to an end, are all closed for the night by order of the marshal, but the streets are lined with festive torches. And the people who fill the square with us—there are thirty or forty of us in all who have been admitted into the Restricted Zone—are buzzing quietly in anticipation.

Maybe it's the masks. What is it about wearing a mask that just amps up the exhilaration? Like you're not really you, I guess—you can just be anyone you want. There's an elephant with a grotesque, rubbery snout swinging down at waist level. There's a yellow-eyed jackal. There are twisted pig faces, white wolves, iridescent dragons, bats and lizard people, prehistoric birds with ghostly white plumage. Tony says the more elaborate ones are custom-made, brought from home by the folks who are lucky enough to get a regular spot in the RZ. But the rentals aren't bad either. Dylan dons his, a fox head with brownish-orange fur and two long, pointed ears. Mine is a brown bear. "Papa Bear," says Dylan, which is delightful. (Maybe my new nickname from Dylan? We'll see!)

At ten forty-five the first notes of the anthem come through the loudspeaker. The square falls silent and we stand at attention and turn to face the courthouse flag. Even Dylan is standing straight, his furry fox face lifted in pride. I'm not exactly a flag-waving type myself, and I've never really shared Dylan's interest in the Parade. But it's almost too adorable.

The anthem comes to an end. I'm expecting a speech or a round of applause but everyone remains silent and still. Clearly this isn't the first Parade for a lot of these folks!

And then out of the quiet and the dark, we hear the calliope. Dylan inches closer to me and actually takes my hand. The music is slow, haunting, dreamlike. I shiver despite the warm night, my arms covered in goosebumps. It really is the stuff memories are made of, I think.

Tapping Dylan's shoulder, I point to the George Washington statue in front of the courthouse, and he nods. We climb the base of the statue and settle in, side by side at Washington's feet, legs hanging over the edge. From here we can see everything as the Parade winds its way through the square.

The music gets louder, and the crowd in the square becomes more animated.

"There," Dylan whispers, seeing the calliope first as it rounds the nearest corner, immediately in front of us, and enters the square. It's unlit except for the large spoked wheels, on which glowing white skulls rotate as they move. In the dark the calliope looks huge and lumbering, something from another, more ancient world.

"Here we go," I say. "Parade Master."

I've seen pictures of the Parade Master but he's a lot more impressive up close. He wears a crow's mask and walks on twenty-foot stilts that bend backward in the middle, like bird legs. He turns his head to look down at us with his dead black eyes as he walks past, making both Dylan and me shiver, and then laugh. Behind him comes a group of smaller crows on foot, each of them with torches, walking together in lockstep like little weird slow-moving patriotic nightmare birds.

Next come the floats. These are festooned with multi-colored lights and fantastical scenes, each more elaborate than the last. Here are dancing skeletons, and three-headed dogs, and angels feasting on the flesh of demons, and traitors swinging from the gallows, and the heathen broken on the wheel, and savages kneeling in supplication before their masters, and the American Jesus descended from the cross to smite the ignorant and the damned. It's all beautiful and strange and uplifting and hopeful and yet gross and unsettling.

Last of all comes the wagon, drawn by two magnificent black horses. The wagon driver steps out, and as he moves around to the back of the wagon, the Parade Master's voice comes over the loudspeaker. Just a reminder to all of us, he says, that being here is a privilege, not a right. Only use the instruments that have been provided, he says. And most importantly, have fun.

The wagon door swings open and the prisoners begin to emerge. They're in black cloaks and hoods, all of them, and many stumble and stagger like zombies as they come out onto the street beneath the torches.

"Why do they move like that?" Dylan asks.

I tell him that a lot of the prisoners are drug addicts.

"That one looks small," he says, pointing. "Like a kid."

I remind him there aren't any kids. Only adults. The worst of the worst. "But it's okay if you feel weird about it. It's probably sort of nice if you feel weird about it."

"I don't." He reaches into his swag bag and withdraws a bat. It's painted black with an American flag emblem along the barrel, beneath the words PROTECT. DEFEND. PLAY BALL. "This is all we get?"

"We're not supposed to really hurt them," I say. "It's a lesson. Or, like, a metaphor." I can't exactly remember the metaphor. Something-something beating back the dark forces of something.

Dylan slides down off the statue as the last of the prisoners emerge into the square. There are about two dozen of them, connected by a long chain attached to their ankles. They shuffle forward as a group, prodded by one of the little crows, until they're in the center of the square. A few make sounds—grunty screamy sounds, nothing particularly intelligent—but most are quiet. I appreciate the quiet ones. Accepting their punishment with some grace, which says a lot about them. When you think about it, I mean.

The Parade Master comes forward on his stilts and reminds us that nobody leaves the square without permission. The masked crowd moves forward, surrounding the prisoners, and Dylan hurries to join them. The little crow goes from prisoner to prisoner and unlocks the ankle chains, then withdraws behind the Parade Master at the edge of the square.

I hang back. My heart's pounding suddenly. I peer down into my bag but I don't remove the bat. I try to think of a prime number.

Dylan turns back to me, expectant.

The calliope music swells, and somewhere a bell rings.

The crowd closes in. The pavement rumbles and the prisoners in their black cloaks disappear under the scrum. In the torchlight I can only see flashes of animal faces, and light glinting off the swinging bats as they arc through the air. The calliope grows louder, and I'm glad, because there's another sound beyond the rumbling, and it's the sound of men and women screaming. And I know it's not the prisoners screaming, but the rest of them, the rest of us.

I ease myself down from the statue right as the first of the prisoners breaks free and stumbles blindly in my direction. My heart thumps and leaps from my throat. Before I have to make a decision, an elephant and a jackal leap forward to take the prisoner down from behind. I turn away then, before they start in with the bats. But there's a sound. Like something is broken. Like something is being split open. Like—

(Two-five-seven-eleven-thirteen-seventeen-nineteen)

I run forward into the square to find Dylan. Everyone is running now, there's no order left at all. The calliope speeds up. Someone is screaming and someone is laughing and it's right next to me or right on top of me and I realize it's just me.

Between the courthouse and a barber shop I spot an alley, and I make my way there to hide and wait for Dylan. I pull my bear mask off and lean my face against the cool brick of the courthouse wall. Just a few seconds. I need just a few seconds to get myself together.

Something moves against my ankle.

One of the prisoners is lying on his side, facing me. His hood has fallen off and dark liquid oozes from a head wound. A wide strip of silver tape covers his mouth, and from the weird angle of his arms I can tell that his hands are bound behind his back under the cloak. He turns his head and looks up at me, eyes wide and alert. Blood bubbles from his mouth.

He looks familiar. He looks, I mean just a little. Probably not. But maybe. It was dark then, and dark now.

My eyes move back to the square. Some in the crowd have assembled in the far corner with the Parade Master, near the calliope. Others are still running around, bats waving, shouting, laughing. The small crows move from place to place, taking a count of the bodies.

I go down to one knee beside the prisoner. "Be silent," I tell him, and he nods. I pull the tape from his mouth, and then remove the cloak. After I untie his hands, I look him in the eyes, and I tell him to run.

My heart's still racing. But in a good way. Yes I'm almost sure it's a good way. I rise and peer out into the square again. Feeling good. Feeling alive. Feeling courageous? Maybe. I almost wish Dylan could've seen it, what I've just done. A lesson from the old man—Papa Bear! A lesson in showing some mercy. Showing some kindness. Like I'm saying: We can be better than this.

My heart soars, and I scan the torch-lit darkness for my little fox.

There's a whoosh of air beside my right ear, and then a burst of pain and light. I drop to my knees and something hits me in the head again.

I don't even feel myself fall.

My ears are ringing. The calliope goes silent. I try to reach for my head to stop the ringing but I can't move my hands, because they're tied behind my back. The little Malaysian man rolls me onto my side and struggles to slide the cloak over my body.

I should scream.

My brain is fuzzy, but I think I should probably scream now.

Then the tape goes over my mouth and the hood comes down. I can feel but not hear his footsteps as he runs off down the alley to escape. The ringing in my ears begins to fade, and the sounds of the calliope return. The hood isn't totally in place, so I can still see a little. I see torches, crows, beasts of all kinds. And across from me in the shadows of the alley, I see another cloaked, hooded figure lying on the pavement, motionless. She's small and I see that she was able to free her hands before she was brought down. One of her arms extends out of the shadows as if she's reaching for the light, and I see that her nails are blue, as blue as a cloudless summer sky. Blood drips down into one of my eyes, blinding me. With the other eye I can see them. I can see them clearly, moving toward me across the square. Elephant, jackal, tiger, snake, dragon, fox. All of them roaring as they come.

Disappearing Act

SOME TIME AGO I got a call out of the blue from a woman named Donna. She said I probably didn't remember her but I'd been friends with her brother Bennie, and she wanted to tell me Bennie was dead. I was at a bar called Sign of the Whale in Pittsburgh when she called. It was a small place, only a couple booths and not much lighting. There were four other people in the bar at the time and I knew all four by name, though I almost never spoke to any of them. It wasn't that kind of bar.

"Bennie," I said. I thought I should know the name of someone whose sister would call to tell me he died. I felt a mild panic, the sort you feel when you've been drinking and you know something's happening that will bother you later but you can't get worked up about it right then. I pushed myself off the bar stool and stepped into the restroom, the only place where I'd be able to make out what she said without having to ask her to say it again a couple times. I was sober enough to not want to ask her to keep repeating things about her dead brother. The restroom had green walls and green doors on the stalls, but they were different shades of green. I asked her how it happened. She said he got sick, was all. She said he was still living in Millwood, and I must have made some sound then, *ahhh ah oh,* because she asked me if I was alright, and I said yes.

I'd known Bennie in the late seventies. My father had moved us—me and the twins, Teddy and Roo—from Indianapolis to Millwood, in the southern part of New Jersey across the river from Philadelphia, after getting an offer for a job that he'd end up losing six months later. If there had ever been a mill in Millwood, it was long gone when we arrived. The town had a bowling alley, a couple diners, a drive-in theater that showed triple-X movies on the weekends to stay in business, and not much more. There were some nice enough houses in the quiet, shaded part of town along the

Delaware River, but most of the people who lived there, including my family and Bennie's, lived on the other side of the old north-south C&A rail line. After my father lost the job that brought him to Millwood, we stuck around. Maybe he thought we needed some stability by then. Maybe he liked the town, despite everything.

I asked Bennie's sister if he'd ever gotten married. She said no. We were quiet for a bit and it was on the tip of my tongue then to ask something that would've sounded dumb. I wanted to ask how her brother's life had been. I didn't know what that would've meant. I guess I wanted to know if he'd done anything surprising. If he'd found someone he loved. If he'd traveled at all. If he'd been delighted by something—if he'd had anything in his life that gave him some kind of grace, maybe, even if it wasn't anything permanent. Especially if it wasn't anything permanent. It seemed important to know that. But I'd only drank enough to think about those things, and not enough to say them out loud. And so all I asked was if he'd ever become a magician, which sounded dumber than all of that.

"A what?" she asked.

"A magician." I had to reach out to the restroom counter to steady myself. "I remember he was into that."

She said she didn't know and had to get going. I asked about the funeral and she said it had already happened. I asked how she'd come across my name and she said he'd left a list. She found me online. I said oh, and then we hung up. I was looking at myself in the restroom mirror as we talked. In the fluorescent light my face was green, like everything else in the room. I thought I looked like a damn ghoul.

I WAS LIVING with a woman named Melissa at the time. She was a waitress with a heart of gold. That's how she introduced herself to me at the bar where I met her: "I'm Melissa and I've got a heart of gold." She said that to everyone. Her schtick. I said well I'm a drifter with a secret past, and she asked if there was any other kind, and that made me smile. A month later I moved in with her. She didn't like me coming around to the bar once we got together so I spent most of my nights in other spots, like Sign of the Whale.

I left the bar after talking to Bennie's sister and went home and poured myself another gin and tonic and took out a pad and paper. I was thinking about Bennie and what I might've said if I had to give a eulogy for him. Probably I was drunk. But I had this thought of how it would begin. I sipped from my glass and I wrote "BENNIE" in all caps at the top, and underlined it a couple or three times, and then below that I wrote these words:

Sleight of hand was what Bennie liked.

That's all I had. I kept drinking and looking down at the paper and maybe I passed out at some point. I heard Melissa come home, heard her getting changed in the bedroom, heard her pour herself a drink. She drank whiskey sours. She sat down next to me and turned the pad toward her. I could smell the whiskey and the smoke and the perfume on her.

"Who's Bennie?" she asked.

I said he was a friend and he was dead, and I was just putting some thoughts down. She asked when the funeral was and I said it already happened. She laughed. She said you're writing a eulogy for a funeral you missed and I said Yeah, and she said You're a stupid fucker ain't you, and I said Yeah, I am.

~

I didn't think of Bennie often after that, but there were a couple times when he came to mind.

One of those times was when I was out in Houston. I was living with another girl then, named Miriam. Melissa and Miriam. This was a couple years later. I used to get them mixed up, the names. It drove Miriam nuts. She said I probably still had a thing for Melissa, and I told her that wasn't it at all, I wasn't even thinking of Melissa by then. I just had trouble pulling the right words and names out sometimes. She said it was because I drank too much and I said that's what Miriam used to say, too. That made her laugh. I could make her laugh sometimes.

Miriam's father had gotten me a job working at his company, which manufactured medical devices. I remember they had a medical screw made partly out of human and cow bones. He hired me on as a project manager even though I didn't know what that was. He said not to worry about it and that I just had to set up meetings and check to make sure everyone else was doing their job. I tried doing that for a while. I wrote down everything anyone said, even though I didn't understand much of it, and then I set up the next meeting for everyone. I quit drinking around then, mostly, because Miriam said I had to. I don't know if that was the reason but my sleep went all to hell. I'd just lie there in bed all night not knowing what to do. Like there was some trick to falling asleep and I'd forgotten how to do it. Some nights I'd forget how to even breathe without thinking about it, and I'd have to stay up just to be sure I kept breathing. Soon I was showing up late for work, and when I was able to keep the meetings I'd set up and not fall asleep in the middle of them, I understood things even less than before. I figured everybody knew I didn't belong there. I started drinking again but just a little, to push that feeling down.

One day I had to walk out of a meeting because I was sweating so much. I thought of asking if anyone else was hot but I didn't want to see to look on their faces if I was wrong and it was only me. Finally when my clothes were soaked through, this woman named Carol or Karen said Jesus maybe you need a minute, and I got up and went to the restroom, thinking I'd throw up and feel better and then I could get back to work. I didn't, though. I kept my face on the toilet seat to cool myself down. After ten minutes I felt sort of okay again. I washed my hands and my face, and then I walked out of the building.

I didn't know my way around that part of Houston, and I only wandered. Warehouses and chain-link fences gave way to a residential neighborhood. At the end of the road I came to a park with a tree-lined walking path that ran along one of the bayous and up toward some lighted ballfields far in the distance. The sky looked like rain and it was a weekday but there was a crowd of maybe a dozen people gathered just inside the park at a picnic area, so I went to see what was happening. A young bearded guy in jeans and a white T-shirt with sunglasses on top of his head was sitting behind a card table. He had a tattoo on his left arm that was partially hidden by the shirt sleeve, but I could see the bottom of it pretty clear. It looked like a wolf's head. I stood back from the group and watched him do the cup and balls trick. He used red Solo cups and three different rubber balls in red, green and blue. His hands were good. I couldn't follow him, anyway. I tried to listen to what he was saying but he mostly mumbled around a cigarette in his mouth. His eyes darted around but never settled on anyone.

I thought I'd start to feel better there in the park but I didn't. Maybe it was just that the air was heavy and I was having trouble drawing a breath. Maybe it was something else. People came and went around the table but I stuck around. He made forty dollars while I stood there. Nobody guessed right.

When the crowd thinned and it was only me, he asked without looking up if I wanted to try, so I stepped forward.

I pointed at his arm even though he couldn't see me. "Your arm," I said. "What's with the wolf?"

He rolled up the sleeve. Above the wolf's head were two words, *Lone Wolf*, tattooed in some fancy calligraphy font.

"That's funny?" He rolled down the sleeve.

Maybe I looked like I was going to laugh, I don't know. I shook my head, feeling lousy. "Your patter," I said. "It's bad."

"Okay." He began gathering his things together.

"Your hands are good but your patter isn't. You mumbled. You didn't look at anybody. The whole point is to get people to look at you."

He ignored me.

I was sweating again and I had a taste in my mouth I didn't like. Metallic, unhealthy. "Thimblerig," I said. "You ought to talk about thimblerig. That's a cool name and you ought to talk about it. People like learning something. That's something you could teach people. What a thimblerig was."

He swept his things into a knapsack and didn't answer.

"From ancient Egypt." My head was pounding now. "You dumb shit."

He stood up. He was a lot bigger standing, but I could see he didn't want any trouble with me. I didn't want any trouble either. He was a kid, was all. But I said, "You ought to care more. About doing it right."

He flipped the table over and leaned down to fold the legs back. Looking up at me, he blinked a couple times and then said, "Jesus, you look sick."

I was about to say that he was the one who was sick, because he couldn't be bothered to learn about fucking thimblerigs and ancient Egypt, and because his tattoo was obvious and embarrassing. Instead I threw up all over the sidewalk. There was some blood in it. He didn't stick around. I felt unsteady so I knelt down on the sidewalk and waited to throw up again, but that was it. I crawled as far as I could make it from where I'd thrown up and curled up on the grass as the rain started to come down through the trees. I remember thinking I was glad it was raining, so the vomit would wash away.

Later I told Miriam about it. She asked what all that was about, and I told her I knew someone once who liked this stuff. She asked what his name was and I said I couldn't remember. She said how was it that I remembered thimblerigs and ancient Egypt but I couldn't remember a person's goddamn name, and so I told her his name was Bennie. She said Okay and then she burst out crying.

I believed, then, that all relationships had a trajectory to them, an upward arc that bent downward over time. That's what I'd figured out. It took me a while. I'd seen that you could look back—you couldn't hardly ever spot it at the time, but you could look back—and just about see the moment when the arc started to bend down. It probably wasn't any big event, a blowout fight or an affair or anything like that. Those things came later. They came because the arc had already started to bend, they came because you'd lost something, depleted some bank of goodwill that you'd built up, the two of you, while you were falling in love. I thought maybe that's all love was, just an accumulation of goodwill that reached a point where it had to expend itself. And when that happened, you'd lose patience a little easier. You'd find a sore spot a little faster. You'd be less generous, less trusting of the other person's motives and heart. And for that reason you'd hold back in countless ways, maybe not even knowing you were holding back, and the arc would bend down even more.

With Miriam, that wasn't the moment. I'd already started running around on her by then. I knew the arc had bent. That was just the moment when she knew it too.

~

BENNIE, NOW. Let me tell you about Bennie.

Bennie was the best magician I ever saw. I met him when he was ten years old. We'd ride our bikes in the summer over the bridge from Millwood to Moorestown and set up in front of the 7-Eleven. We had a deal with the manager, fifteen percent off the top. Bennie would hang a banner from the table, "The Astonishing Maldini," and most days he'd have a crowd of three or four teens, maybe a parent or two, or a teacher broadcasting vague disapproval, throughout the afternoon. He did card tricks, vanishing quarters, Slydini's handkerchief knots. Those knots were his favorite. I made fun of him for the name—"Maldini," I said, what the hell is that, your name's Malden, and he said you got to have a name that ends with an "i." Houdini, Slydini. Anyway he'd sit there and pass two handkerchiefs back and forth between his smooth hands, doing his weird low-key patter—*that's a square knot, right there, my granddad taught me that knot before he died but maybe you could check it out for me, sir.* He never even knew either of his grandfathers. He was a quiet kid, even with me, but when he was dealing, somehow he could talk. Somehow when he was dealing he was the smoothest kid you ever saw. The handkerchief thing drove me nuts. I'd have to remind him, riding over, to switch to the cup and balls before too long, since that's where the money was. Nobody gave a damn about those knots. They'd stare at him and maybe they'd say how the hell did you do that, but they didn't give up anything for it. Ten minutes into the cup and balls routine, I'd show up and win a few dollars, and that would get things rolling. But I only won because I was the stooge. If Bennie didn't want me to find the ball, I wasn't going to find it. Nobody was going to find that damn ball. Chance would tell you somebody should've found the ball once a while, without even trying, but they never did. Like he had some real magic going on, useless but benign. And maybe that's the only kind of magic that's worth anything.

Now this is an old game, one of the oldest, going back to ancient times so they say. In Egypt they called it thimblerig, which is a funny name but they called it that because they played it with thimbles. Some folks will say it's all trickery and maybe that's true but my grandmother taught me this version here and she didn't have any trickery in her so we'll just start things off nice and slow, you see this here rubber ball that is an ordinary rubber ball in every single respect. And why don't you pick it up just to test it out for me, thank you, and I think you'd agree that there's no black magic in that ball, it's as a real as you and me. . . .

I was a kid myself so I never thought to ask where that came from, how an eleven-year-old kid in New Jersey could talk like that. Maybe Bennie didn't even know himself. Maybe he read about it somewhere. I never knew anyone who read so much. Once when I was bored I dragged Bennie with me to the mall to steal something. I said it could be anything at all as long as we each picked something and went through with it. I grabbed a shaving kit from the Macy's, thinking it was a fine thing to steal because I couldn't shave yet but I'd be able to someday. When it was Bennie's turn, we walked around the plaza until he stopped in front of the bookstore. He went in, then came out a few minutes later with a copy of *Moby-Dick* under his shirt. I figured he was the only person who ever lived who'd shoplift a book. Much less *Moby-Dick*. "Plus I thought you read that already," I said to him, and he said, "Yeah, I did."

Another time we hitchhiked from Millwood to the Jersey Shore. It was toward the end of the school year, late May. The police had been called out to Bennie's house that week and I could tell he was out of sorts even if he didn't say much about what happened. He never talked about what went on at home. I knew he'd been pulled out of the house a couple times before I moved to town, but only because I'd heard it from some other kids at school. They said his parents were violent drunks, or meth dealers, or cult members, or maybe it was Bennie himself who was the crazy one. Nobody really knew anything. I should have asked him to tell me but I didn't. Maybe he was quiet when we were together, but he seemed happy much of the time. And when he wasn't happy, like that Saturday in May, I came up with things like hitchhiking to Wildwood. That's all I knew how to do.

I remember it was a pretty day, bright and warm but not too hot to be comfortable. We spent most of it hunting for treasure under the boardwalk, and talked. Mostly I talked. Bennie wasn't into the things I talked about, but he'd listen and he'd ask me questions. He'd ask if I thought Bruce Lee could beat Muhammad Ali, and who was having a good season for the Phillies this year, and how I'd rank all the horror movies I'd ever seen. And I'd answer, and he'd think about that too.

When the light was falling and it was about time to head back, Bennie said he'd been thinking about a place called Emerald Isle. We were lying on the sand, shirtless under the warm sun and that pretty sky, a block north of the boardwalk. Daytrippers were heading home and we were mostly by ourselves. I asked Bennie what he liked about Emerald Isle and how he'd found it. He said he found it on a map and he'd been thinking it sounded like a nice place to live someday. I asked what was wrong with New Jersey and he said he didn't want to spend his whole life in New Jersey. Too much had happened in New Jersey already, he said. And he liked the sound of Emerald Isle. He liked that nobody had heard of it. He said maybe when we were older I could come visit him there. I said sure. I asked if he'd be working as a magician then and he said no. He said maybe he'd be working on a boat. Not doing anything special, he said, just taking people out on a boat during the day, maybe teaching them how to sail after he learned how to sail. I pictured him out on the water, teaching people in that quiet voice of his. I figured he'd know everything there was to know about sailing by then if that's what he wanted to do, and I said that sounded fine. He said he was glad to hear me say that, and then he brushed his hand against mine in the sand like he was trying to hold it. I pulled away and climbed to my feet and ran into the ocean. Bennie stayed on the beach. When I turned and started back toward the shore he was on his feet, pulling his shirt back on, and before long we headed back home.

Not long after that, Bennie went up to Teaneck to live with his aunt and uncle. Kids said it was because he'd tried to do something crazy, like hang himself or set the house on fire. Nobody else knew him too well, so I guess anything seemed possible. Kids liked to tell stories. We had no way of knowing for sure. I didn't say anything. I could have, but I didn't. After a while people stopped talking about him.

At the beginning of our junior year he came back. I'd grown four inches and added thirty pounds by then. Bennie looked the same. Maybe a little taller, his face a little more withdrawn. Still too thin, too fragile somehow. When I saw him in the hallways I nodded, sometimes. Other times I looked right through him as if we'd never known each other at all. He didn't call me out on it. He'd just keep walking when I did that, like it wasn't any big deal, like it wasn't some kind of test I'd just faced and failed, even if I knew it was. Funny how you can know a thing like that. Even as a kid, you can know it.

I live, now, in a small house outside of Charleston, with a woman named Janey. When the weather's good at the end of the day I sit outside and watch the sun glint off the marshes of Clark Sound, same as everyone else, and then go back inside. When the weather's bad I stay outside longer. Maybe because I'm the only one out there, and that appeals to me. Maybe because I think someone ought to be out there to be a witness. Otherwise what's the point.

My job these days is managing a small office supply warehouse. I started out as a driver, running shipments to stores from Charleston up to Rocky Mount, and I guess I stuck around long enough that they asked me to run things. I said that was okay with me but I still wanted to drive sometimes, so about once a month I get in the company truck at seven in the morning and drive north. I spend the hours on the road inside my head, a place I'm not used to spending much time. When I get so that I need to talk to someone, which is more often than I'd expect, I call Janey.

I told Janey early on about the arc. I said it wasn't a terrible thing to know but that I'd come to know it. We were in her kitchen. She had a nice apartment she was living in then, small but nice. She'd come out of a divorce and was trying to put a life together for herself. When I was finished talking she put her head in her hands and sort of laughed, or made some sound anyway. She asked where we were in the arc and I said I didn't know. She said maybe that's why you're telling me this now and I agreed, maybe it was. She asked if I was in love with her and I said I didn't know, I didn't even know how to tell if I was in love anymore. What it would feel like. I only knew that my soul was quiet when I was with her, and she said that sounds like a good start.

Driving down from Rocky Mount one day in early September I saw a billboard showing a grassy beach, empty except for a pair of old bicycles leaning against a wooden fence, below a sky as pretty and blue as anything I'd ever seen. I must have passed it dozens of times, coming and going. I'd never paid attention to the words on the billboard before, but this time I took notice.

COME HOME TO EMERALD ISLE

CROWN JEWEL OF THE CRYSTAL COAST

I didn't know what I was doing until I'd come to a stop on the shoulder. I shut off the ignition and looked up at the billboard and read the words again, and dropped my hands from the steering wheel into my lap. I felt strange. Like I couldn't move, or like I'd somehow reached the end of something and now I didn't know where to go. After a bit I called Janey. I told her where I was and I said I just needed to sit for a while. I said I got reminded of someone and it was a long time ago and I just needed to sit. I didn't plan to tell her about Bennie but I did anyway, or some of it. My thoughts were scattered. I said he was the best magician I ever knew and I was supposed to meet up with him in Emerald Isle someday, but he was long dead now.

She was quiet while I talked. Quiet but still there. Some people you can tell are still with you even when they're not saying anything. When I was done, she said, "You should go there."

It was getting late and I still had a couple hours left to drive home. "Someday," I said.

"Go," she said. "Commune. And come back to me."

I didn't have an answer to that, and she wouldn't have accepted one anyway. So I left the interstate, and drove east.

A two-lane highway took me through a state park before opening, after a long time, to a causeway leading to the island. There was no grand sign announcing Emerald Isle. As if you weren't supposed to find it unless you were looking for it. It was a quiet place, full of trees, with a path running alongside the main road that was full of people and dogs and bikes despite the hour. None of the big hotels lining the beach that I remembered from New Jersey as a boy. But I lowered the window and took in the sea air and it was like childhood itself, like finding something I never knew I'd lost, or thrown aside.

I found a spot to park outside a condominium complex and called Janey to tell her I'd made it. The sun was mostly down by then and it was end-of-summer cool when I opened the car door. I followed a winding road through the complex until I came to a wooden bridge leading over the dunes to the beach.

I left my shoes behind on the bridge and walked out on the sand. Clouds and the late hour had chased most everyone else away, and the wind was picking up. Far off I could hear the shorebirds crying. I thought about what Janey said, but I knew it wasn't in me to do that. To commune. That sounded sacred. I thought that whatever part of me might have been able to do that had been used up long ago. I couldn't even remember all that I wanted to remember. I didn't even have that to offer. So I only stood still and watched the surf, and listened, until I knew it was time to go. The light was gone by then. And there was no one left but me.

Jellyfish

WE AWOKE AND DRESSED in the dark, then grabbed our pillows and climbed like ghosts into the back seat of the car. Still half-asleep but jockeying for position, drawing silent battle lines against the dawn. A light rain was falling. Walt: is it going to rain the whole time? I don't know. But what's the point of—I don't know, I don't know what to tell you. It won't rain the whole time. But you just said—Me, interrupting: when is Dad coming? Walt kicked me then and we left the driveway as I tried not to cry. I was asleep by the time we made it to the interstate, a one-eyed bear held together with masking tape standing guard between Walt and me. When I woke up we were at the beach, heavy salt air and sound of gulls crying overhead, and the rain was gone. Our mother set up the umbrella and Walt and I went down to the water, and Walt shrieked Jellyfish heads, jellyfish heads. They were scattered everywhere along the sand like sea glass. We scooped them up and threw them, back into the sea and at each other, war-cries ringing in the ocean air, and she sat on the blanket and watched us while sunlight bounced off her sunglasses. We built a castle with a moat and I found a scrap of driftwood to use as a drawbridge. Walt beamed, then disappeared while I shored up the walls, and when he returned he was carrying four sticks. He placed the sticks at the four corners of the castle, and then impaled a jellyfish head on each—a warning to the others, he said. Our mother walked past us, invisible. When we finally looked up and saw her she was twenty yards out to sea. Walt took another jellyfish and sliced it in two with a penknife he'd swiped from the junk drawer. A sacrifice, he said. I looked up and down the beach. Where are all the tentacles? He shrugged. Out there, he said, meaning the sea, but his head was down, everything forgotten except the sacrifice. I stood and scanned the ocean. At first there was nothing. Then I saw her, farther out, her white swimsuit flashing like a diamond in a magician's hand: there, and then gone again. Years later she said she had no memory of turning back, seeing me on the shore next to a castle fortified with jellyfish heads. I raised my hand and waved. Walt: the moat has to be deeper, this is a fucking bullshit moat. She disappeared again, and when she reappeared she was farther out, gaining on the horizon. There were clouds coming in from the north, and August was ending.

Cary Grant at the Orpheum Theatre

ONE SATURDAY I FOUND my mother sitting at the end of the third row along the aisle when I went in to clean up before the matinees. She wore a pale lavender dress and her hair was tied with a yellow ribbon. The ribbon was ghost-white in the screenglow, but I knew it was yellow. I remembered her wearing it every day one summer. She told us she just woke up and decided she wanted to be the kind of person who wore a ribbon in her hair. My mother was like that.

"They don't make them like Cary Grant anymore," she said, when I came down front to sweep. "Don't you think, Will?"

I turned my head toward the screen. *North by Northwest* was running because I didn't like when the theater was all quiet, and because I liked Cary Grant. Right now he was drinking a cocktail on the Twentieth Century Limited with Eva Marie Saint, wearing a suit and sunglasses, while the police searched the train for him. I watched for a minute, and then I started sweeping. I didn't answer my mother. Usually she went quiet if I ignored her long enough.

"Why do you think that is?" she said. "You think people are so different now?"

"..."

"Well I think they're different. Even movie stars are different. Less grand. Smaller than when I was a girl. They're just regular people now."

"..."

I wasn't watching her, I'd moved up the aisle a few rows, but I heard a long sigh coming from her direction.

"Here's a fact," she said. "He wasn't even really named Cary Grant. Did you know that, Will?"

Of course I did know that. I knew a bunch of things about him. Like I knew he was born in England, and his parents were named Elias and Elsie. I knew his brother died of tuberculosis. I knew he'd gotten himself kicked out of school so he could join a vaudeville group and travel. I knew he'd been an acrobat when he was young. I knew he'd been married a bunch of times, and that he was depressed a lot. I'd read a book about him.

"Archibald Leach—that name didn't fit him," said my mother. "But I always felt—this is true—like Cary Grant was his real name somehow. Like he *found* his real name, I mean, even though it was made up."

"..."

She was silent for a bit while I swept. Then: "I wonder if we all have secret names like that. Real names that we're supposed to just *find*."

"..."

"Isn't that kind of a grand idea, Will? And something's missing if we don't find it, even if we don't know it was something we were supposed to be looking for."

I stopped cleaning and watched her from behind, not saying anything. But I liked Archie better. I thought a kid named Archie was someone you'd want to hang around. A kid named Archie would have an embarrassing laugh. He'd wear thick glasses and he'd have a few cowlicks and he'd get mustard and other condiments on his shirt all the time. And you'd think he'd be clumsy and graceless, but you'd be wrong. He'd surprise you by how agile he was, like for example you'd be playing *Sorry!* or *Parcheesi* and he'd all of a sudden get up and do a perfect handstand, and hold it, and then kick over with a backflip to land on his feet. And you'd shake your head and say Damn, Archie, where'd that even come from, and he'd smile this kind of embarrassed smile, like he appreciated the compliment but he regretted the backflip all the same, because it was a little showoffy. Then he'd change the subject. That's who Archie was.

My mother didn't say anything more until I was about finished and walking up the aisle toward the door. Then she called out, "Hey, Will?"

I didn't turn. But something shaky and different in her voice caught me, and I said, "Yeah?" Gooseflesh spread over my arms, and I stopped breathing. I didn't know what she'd say next, but I thought it might be important. It felt like one of those moments in a movie when something big was about to happen.

But all she said was, "Next time let's do *Notorious*."

I let out my breath.

"I so love Ingrid Bergman," she said. "Nothing against Eva Marie Saint, even though she was a blonde. She was Edie Doyle in *On the Waterfront* and she was fine, I thought, even though she had to work with that monster. But Bergman was on another level, wasn't she? And her beauty was so *effortless.* That's real beauty when you don't even have to try to be beautiful. You know your father used to say—"

"Yeah I know," I said, and I walked out.

I went to the projection booth and shut down *North by Northwest*, which still had a few minutes left on the reel. That wasn't friendly but I wasn't in the mood to be friendly. Plus I had to get things set up for the matinee anyway. We were running a Billy Wilder double feature. I slid the Hitchcock reel into the canister and carried it to the storage room. When I opened the door, I found four pairs of eyes blinking at me in the dark from under some old navy blankets in the corner.

Russell was at his desk when I found him, finishing up a phone call.

"I recognize that," he said. "Can't argue with that, no. Even so." He lifted his head and saw me, put out his hand as if I was about to interrupt even though I wasn't. "No. Nope, no problem at all," he said. Then he set down the phone.

The story I was told, growing up, was that Russell bought the theater for my mother. He was older than my mother by a good bit, and for a time he ran a used bookshop in Swedesboro, where she grew up and where they met. They fell for each other despite the age difference, and were married before too long. Edgewood wasn't far, but they likely wouldn't have settled there, and Russell wouldn't have sold his bookshop, if it weren't for the Orpheum. My mother grew up loving the Orpheum. The theater was built long before she was born, back when theaters were more extravagant, even theaters in small New Jersey towns. The big front doors were etched glass, the trim inside was all gleaming copper, and silk curtains covered the screen. Across the dome was a hand-painted mural of Orpheus ascending from the underworld. At least that's how it used to be. By the time Russell and my mother were married, the Orpheum was just barely holding on. The silk curtains were long gone, the glass doors replaced with wood, the mural faded almost to the point of being invisible. The lobby interior was smoke-discolored from a fire in '71 that had almost taken out the whole building. A developer was going to buy the land and put in a service station and convenience store. My mother was heartbroken about it, and I guess

Russell was crazy back then, because he decided to buy it himself and try to turn things around.

"Who was that?" I said.

"Who?" He started going through his desk drawers like he was hunting for something.

I sighed. "On the phone?"

"Oh, oh," he said. "Just business, just the usual."

"Not interested enough to ask what that means," I said. "Anyway we've got raccoons."

He turned away from the desk and opened the bottom drawer of the file cabinet, started pawing through folders.

"Russell," I said. "Raccoons. Live ones. In the storage room."

"Yes, yes," he said.

"There's a hole in the ceiling. I figure there's got to be another hole somewhere in the crawl space where they're getting in."

"Right. Probably," he said. He stopped and slid out one of the folders, thumbed it open. Then he said, "Nope, nope," and slid it back, continuing his search.

"Damn it, Russell."

He turned and blinked at me like he was trying to remember what we'd been just been talking about. "Connie will take care of it," he said. "He's supposed to be here this week to fix the platter."

"He was supposed to be here two weeks ago," I said. Connie was Russell's brother. "We need somebody reliable."

"Connie's reliable."

"If they get into the reels somehow," I said, "it'll kill us." We kept a month's worth of reels in the storage room, rotating in whatever we got from the distributor and sending back the old reels. Lost or damaged reels were expensive.

"I'll call Connie again."

"Now?"

"Soon, soon."

I sighed, and when I did, I thought about how we had the same sigh, me and her. "She was here this morning," I said, "just by the way."

He stopped what he was doing finally, for real this time. "Yeah?" Without looking at me, though.

"Up front, third row."

"She likes that seat." He ran his fingers through his hair, which was thinning and already going gray. He was forty-six. "You talk to her?"

"I said 'Yeah,' I think."

"How'd she look?"

"Like she always looked, I don't know."

"Right," he said.

I didn't like the far-off look in his eyes, so I said, "Maybe you ought to say something to her."

"Maybe I will," he agreed.

But he wouldn't, any more than he'd call Connie.

The first month or so, after she began showing up, neither of us would admit we'd seen her. He'd ask me how things went when I finished sweeping up, and I'd say How do you mean, they went fine, and he'd say Sure, of course. Or during the week when I was at school he'd come home after shutting down the place and he'd look dazed, and I'd ask if he'd seen anything funny to make him look that way, and he'd say No, nothing *funny*, and I'd say Well, anything out of the ordinary then? And he'd say Well, I can't know what you consider ordinary, and I'd say, That's fair enough, and he'd say Unless you had some particular out of the ordinary thing in mind? And I'd say Not exactly a particular thing, no, and we'd go on with our business. Then one day we walked into the small kitchen behind the concession stand and we found her eating from a box of Charleston Chews and reading *The Hollywood Reporter*. Russell dropped his coffee mug and it shattered on the black and white checkered tile floor. He looked at me and then we both looked at her, and she said, *I'm sorry I just really needed some Charleston Chews*. Russell's face was shining.

Since then, he tells me when he sees her, and I tell him. I think neither one of us knows what to do with it, though. He knows I don't like her around. And I know he'll never tell her to leave.

We ended up with a dozen people for the first movie, *Double Indemnity*. All the regulars, like Mr. Solazzo who was a failed movie director before he became an English teacher, and the entire eight-woman Edgewood Bridge Club, plus a pair of film students who took the bus here from the city. Plus there was Todd, who was in my class at school. He wasn't a regular.

His soccer game had been rained out so he needed something to do. He brought a free pass that he said his sister won in a raffle over the summer.

"You even got digital?" he asked, tearing a Twizzler apart with his teeth.

I snatched the pass and said, "You ain't paying anyway. Plus it's better than digital because it's the real thing."

"Delray 6 has digital."

"Sounds like Paradise," I said. "You should check it out."

He blinked at me and glanced around. "Smells like meningitis in here. I bet you've got the meningitis here, like, really bad."

"That's just stupid," I said. "And you're not supposed to bring your own candy in, everybody knows that."

"What's this movie even about?" He was still chewing, with his head tilted up at the film poster now. "I never even heard of it. They spelled *identity* wrong too. Why don't you guys show new stuff? No wonder you're going out of business. That's what my dad says."

I handed him back the free pass. "Sorry," I said. "Movie's cancelled."

"But people are still going in. I see Mr. Solazzo."

"Cancelled for you," I said. "Go on, get out."

I was roping off the entrance when Elizabeth showed up. Elizabeth was younger than me by a couple of years. She was wearing an oversized ratty blue dress with white daisies, and as always she looked just a little dirty. Her mousy hair was damp from the rain because she didn't like umbrellas.

She blinked up at me. Her eyes were too big for her head, and when she blinked it just made them look even bigger somehow. "I fell a couple times on the way over," she said, "which is why I'm late. I scraped my elbow too."

"Didn't ask for your life story," I said.

She started hunting through a change purse attached to a chain she carried over her shoulder. "I think I got enough. I helped Milly on her paper route this week."

"Just go on in," I said, and I waved her through. "God damn."

"Thanks, Will," she said. "I'll be in the balcony this time, on the left."

"Like I needed to know that," I said.

I went back to the booth and got the movie going. After that I vacumed the lobby, locked the concession door, and told Russell to keep an eye on things. When I went back into the theater, I slid down into the seat next to Elizabeth in the balcony. By then, Fred MacMurray was recording a long message for Edward G. Robinson, confessing to murder.

Elizabeth leaned her head toward me. "I know I'm not supposed to say anything," she whispered.

"Then don't."

"But I don't get it."

"Just watch," I said.

"I know who the murderer is," she said.

"We all do."

"Okay."

She was mostly silent for the rest of it. Now and then she'd brush her arm against mine. She told me once that she did that to make sure she wasn't dead. That was my fault. I'd told her that the first time she came to the theater, I thought she was the ghost of a little drowned girl, just because of how she looked. That would've been more interesting than the truth, which was that she was just pale and lonely. She lived with her grandparents because her parents were both in and out of rehab all the time. At least once a year, she said, one or the other of them showed up and tried to convince her to run off with them, even though the courts said she was better off with her grandparents. She worried about things a lot, and now she worried sometimes that she was actually dead and didn't know it, so she'd come up with reasons to bump against me. Once she had me practice handshaking with her because she said she felt like she needed to work on her grip, but I knew the reason.

I left before the ending so I could open the concessions back up, while Russell took care of the booth and got the reels ready for *The Apartment*, the second half of the double feature. While I was out in the lobby I spotted a man standing out front, squinting up at the marquee in a light rain. He was bald and thin, so thin I that could make out the exact shape of his skull, all the individual bumps and ridges. I thought maybe he was coming for the second movie, but he was dressed too well, in a dark gray suit. All he did was walk around the building, twice. Then he went and sat with the wipers running in his car, a black Oldsmobile sedan with yellow-gold Pennsylvania plates.

When *The Apartment* ended, Elizabeth helped me get the place cleaned up and ready to hand off to Russell for the evening shows. By the time we stepped outside the rain had stopped and it was growing dark. The Oldsmobile was still in the parking lot.

A thought occurred to me, and I asked Elizabeth if she saw a black sedan in the lot.

She was unlocking her bike from the rack, but stopped and stood, and peered in the general vicinity of the lot. "I can't see a dang thing," she said. Then she unzipped her little purse and pulled from it a pair of thick glasses with bright yellow rims, slipped them on. "Yeah I see it now," she said.

"Why the hell would you watch movies without your glasses?" I asked.

She shrugged at me. "I like it fuzzy sometimes. Can use my imagination then." Turning back toward the sedan, she said, "Who's in there?"

"Thought maybe it was Death," I said.

"Oh," she said. "You said Russell's test was. Something, I can't remember."

"Benign."

"You said that's good."

"Maybe he's not here for Russell."

"Yeah, maybe not. Spooky."

"Zip your damn coat up," I said. "No reason to give him a head start."

She smiled at that, but zipped up. "I'll see you next week, Will."

I was planning to ride straight home myself to beat the early sunset. But I liked the smell of the town after the rain, and I liked the look of the sky, gunmetal bleeding into burnt gold at the horizon. So I kept riding.

Edgewood isn't but a dozen blocks from its western to eastern end, and not much bigger north to south. The town is wedged between a highway to the east and the wooded slopes of the Delaware River to the west. Until the late Sixties it was known for the Orpheum and for an old brick building along the riverbank called Trembley House, where supposedly George Washington stayed with his family and some of his officers during the Revolutionary War. People used to come and visit the house, and they'd stay in town and buy crafts and have lunch and funnel cake and do walking tours and so on. Only it turned out Washington never really stayed there, or at least there was some controversy about it that led to the Edgewood Historical Society disbanding and the signs being taken down. People mostly stopped coming to Edgewood, and moving to Edgewood, as a result.

All that was before I was born. We learned about it in school. And so I thought of Edgewood, mostly, the same way I thought of Zell's Wonderland. Zell's was an amusement park halfway between Edgewood and Trenton, and it shut down in '75, not long after Six Flags opened in Jackson. I only knew of it because Russell used to take me to Trenton sometimes for a model train convention. I didn't like model trains but I thought he did, and I guess he had the same thought about me, so once a year, until I was eleven and confessed that I hated everything about model trains, we'd drive to Trenton together and look at trains and pretend to be interested. On the way, we always passed the sign for Zell's. The sign was rusted and half-hidden by tree branches, and the gates to the park, almost buried in the brush, had been chained up for years. But through the trees, in the winter at least, you could just make out the skeleton of an old wooden roller coaster rising toward the sky. I bet that coaster was the biggest one in this part of the state back when Zell's opened. I bet people were excited to come and see it, counted the miles until they saw that sign off the highway. Anyway, people still lived in Edgewood, worked in Edgewood, died in Edgewood. But the town was disappearing into the forest all the same. It was just taking some time.

That pretty late-day sunlight was fading as I made my way up Battlement Hill, which marked the town's southern border with Delray. Battlement was the only good hill in Edgewood, and I usually saved it for the tail end of my ride, when I was already getting tired, because I liked how it made my legs burn and my heart thump.

Tonight I stopped at the crest and caught my breath, and turned my bike around to look down on the town from the middle of the street. Everything was still and silent. No cars moved through the streets, no wind shook the trees. But I could hear the blood racing through my body and I could see my breath plume in the cool air. I waited at the top until the sun disappeared for good, and then I went home.

I CAME TO the theater the next Saturday and found the black sedan back in the lot, parked beside Russell's station wagon.

Voices were coming from Russell's office when I went inside, but the door was closed and I couldn't make anything out. If the thin bald man wasn't Death, I thought maybe he was from the bank, which seemed like more or less the same thing to me. Either way, I didn't think his visit could mean anything good for us.

Their voices grew louder, and they both laughed. The door opened and I stepped back into the kitchen, where I watched discreetly as Russell saw him out.

"From the bank?" I asked, when he returned to his office.

"The bank?" His face was puzzled. "Oh, no, no," he said, with a kind of dismissive wave. "Well. I mean yes, I guess in a way, but not—not like that."

"Meaning?"

He started to speak, then stopped and shrugged. "He wasn't here to collect. He wanted to buy the place."

This was far enough outside what I thought was possible that it took me a minute to process it. "And?" I said, at last.

"Well I turned him down," Russell said.

"Because he didn't offer enough to pay back the loans," I guessed.

"Oh, no," he said. "The amount was fine. He said we needed to clean it up a bit, paint the back wall to cover the graffiti. Nothing unreasonable."

"How much?"

"Will, that's not, it doesn't matter."

"Just tell me."

He shook his head slowly. "It wasn't the money, Will."

"But tell me anyway."

So he told me. I didn't handle the books and I didn't know how much Russell owed on the place, and I didn't know a damn thing about money or how much a lot of money was. But it sounded like a lot.

"That face," he said. "Will, I said I wasn't looking to sell."

I blinked at him. "We could go—anywhere. We could go to Illinois." I'd been reading about Chicago and I thought it sounded like a fine place to go. "We could go to *California.*"

Again, that puzzled look from Russell. Like the thought had really never occurred to him. "But why?" he asked.

"That is the craziest question any person has ever asked," I said, "or ever will ask, or ever could ask. And you know it." I stepped to his office window and glanced out toward the empty lot, all cracked asphalt and weeds. A string of empty billboards dotted the horizon across the highway from the Orpheum. They'd been empty for as long as I could remember. "Jesus, Russell. What's even here for us?"

"You'll get out soon enough," he said, quietly. "A few more years. What's the hurry?"

I didn't know the answer to that. But the empty billboards bothered me more, right then, than Russell turning down an offer on the Orpheum. All I could think to say was that everything here was broken.

"It's not, though," he said. "It's just that it feels that way this time of year." When I didn't answer or even look over at him, he added, "Everything will come back. You'll see."

I left to get things ready for the day. I was too angry to be bothered with loading a reel to watch while I cleaned, so the screen stayed dark. She was there anyway, sitting on the opposite side this time, head upturned to watch a movie that wasn't even playing.

She didn't speak for the longest time. And I had this thought, as I was finishing, that if I turned in her direction now, the seat would be empty. It just felt like things were winding down. She was a projection, that was all, and the bulb had to burn out sooner or later.

But she was still there. Facing me, now.

"I couldn't help that I got sick," she said.

It was strange to have her look right at me. She never did that, and it unsettled me. "But you didn't," I said. "Not really." I wasn't even angry.

"Lost, then," she said.

I turned away and headed up the aisle toward the doors, jasmine everywhere.

"Can't a person just be lost?" she called out. "Will? Can't they?"

THE FIRST TIME she ran off, I was the only one who knew she'd gone anywhere. I found a note in my lunchbox, a sheet of lavender stationery folded neatly in half and lying across a peanut butter and jelly sandwich. The note smelled like jasmine perfume and strawberry Pop Tarts. She had to get her head right, she said in the note. She said it wasn't anybody's fault, although maybe some of it was Russell's fault, but mostly it was nobody's fault. She said she wasn't sure she could be a mother because she didn't know how she was supposed to feel about anything, and it scared her, and her own mother had been the same and she didn't want to end up that way, a mother who thought about terrible things, and so she was going off to figure it all out. She said she loved me and loved Russell too, in her own way. She dated the note and signed it *Valerie (Mom)* and drew a heart under her name. I read the note twice. Then I folded it neatly and slid it back into the lunchbox next to the uneaten food, walked out of the school, and ran the four blocks back to our house. I found her in her bedroom, in a yellow dress with her hair tied up with a matching yellow ribbon, sitting on the bed next to an open suitcase. She told me to sit next to her on the bed, and then she explained that she was okay, she was back and she wasn't going anywhere, and she was sorry about the note. I asked if she meant what she said about not knowing how she was supposed to feel, and she said maybe, but it didn't matter. She asked me not to say anything to Russell, and so I didn't. I was eleven and I didn't know anything.

The second time was a month later. She was gone for a whole weekend. I told Russell then about the note she'd left for me, and about how she'd made me promise not to tell him. We got in the car and he drove us all over Edgewood, looking for her. I didn't know what we were looking for exactly, and I don't know if Russell knew either. On Monday morning she called from a payphone in Youngstown, two towns south of Edgewood, and said she wanted to come home. So we went to get her, and we brought her home. But I knew then that it wasn't permanent. I'd seen enough movies and read enough stories to know that everything happened in threes.

And the third time, she didn't come back.

Spring was close and the days were getting longer, and I figured I would spend time after school each day doing what I could to fix things up. Maybe the black Oldsmobile wouldn't return, but I thought someone else might, and maybe Russell could be persuaded. So I painted over the graffiti on the back wall, and cleared out the broken glass and other debris from the alley beside the parking lot, and tightened the door handles inside and out, and replaced the four bulbs in the marquee that had been burned out since the month after she left for good.

Connie came by to fix the platter, which had been causing us problems for months, and to help with the raccoons. I liked Connie despite what I said to Russell. He was the older of the two, but he'd never had a steady job and never gotten married. A month before his high school graduation, he dropped out of school and ran off with a friend who got him a gig as a roadie for a metal band that was going on tour in Canada. He did that for a while, and then he was an electrician's apprentice somewhere in New England, and then he worked construction jobs down in Florida. Now and then he returned to Edgewood, for a day or a week, usually with a new tattoo that he couldn't remember getting. Sometimes he'd take me fishing or kayaking or hiking through the Pine Barrens, and then he was gone again, and nobody would hear from him for months. Until one day he showed up in town and said he was back for good. He rented a room from an old friend who still lived in town, and traveled around the southern part of the state doing odd jobs wherever he found them. But he stuck around.

I showed him the storage room. The raccoons had retreated to the crawl space by then, so he patched the hole in the ceiling. He wanted to set traps in the crawl space, but I wouldn't let him.

"They're humane," he said. "The traps, I mean." Then he scratched his head, and said, "Kind of. Won't kill them, anyway."

I said no. I said the mother might hurt herself trying to break free, or one of the kits might get trapped.

Connie thought about it. "We could drive them out," he said after a bit. Raccoons liked quiet nests, he said. Quiet and dark. We settled on rigging the crawl space with a mini flashlight and an AM radio that played sports talk all day. I'd check on things and replace the batteries every couple of days, and Connie would come back in two weeks to see if we'd run them off, and then he'd run hardwire mesh over the vents and any other gaps to keep them out for good.

When we were done, I stood with him out back and watched him smoke a cigarette. His eyes were far-off, as if he was thinking about somewhere else. Or maybe it's just that I was thinking about somewhere else.

I asked him why he came back.

He smiled without looking at me. "How many times you planning to ask me that question?"

"You won't ever tell me," I said.

"Well, I like the sound the streetlamps make when they come on at night," he said.

"If you looked at me you'd know I'm rolling my eyes."

He laughed softly, and said, "Yeah, I hear 'em." He dropped the cigarette, stamped it out with his foot, then leaned down to retrieve the stub and slide it into the front pocket of his jeans. "How's your dad doing?"

"Like I'd know," I said. Which was true but I didn't like how it sounded, as if I was being flip. So I said, "Maybe he's alright. Most days he's okay. He won't talk about things, so I can't tell."

Connie nodded. "Guess we're all like that. Thought maybe you'd be the one to break it."

"Break what?" I asked.

He slid his hands in his pockets. "The spell," he said. "Whatever spell it is, I don't know. Keeps us from talking."

"It's no damn spell," I said. "It's just stubborn."

"Right." He nodded at this, to himself, like we'd just resolved something. "You guys still seeing her in there?"

"Not really." I'd regretted telling Connie about her almost from the minute the words left my mouth.

That drew another quiet laugh, though not an unkind one. "Right," he said again. "Well I'm not trained in exorcisms anyway, so I guess that's a good thing." He reminded me to check the batteries in the crawl space and to call him if the raccoons took off, and then he left.

Spring came. The raccoons stuck around despite the flashlight and the radio, so I figured maybe Connie didn't know what he was talking about. Or maybe there was something about the place they just liked. Either way I decided they weren't causing any real harm now. I stopped changing the batteries.

We ran a pair of Ingrid Bergman films the first weekend in March. The distributor was supposed to send *Spellbound* and *Anastasia* but the order got crossed up, so instead of *Spellbound* we got *Notorious* instead. Maybe because it was finally nice outside after a long stretch of cold and rainy weather, no one but Elizabeth showed up to watch. Usually we stopped the projector after fifteen minutes if we didn't get at least one paying customer, but I could tell Elizabeth was into *Notorious* right away. I didn't even mind explaining the story to her, since our talking wasn't bothering anyone.

"She's the one who looks like your mom," she said.

"Maybe," I said.

"She's beautiful."

"I guess."

"Did your dad used to look like him?"

"Cary Grant?"

"Yeah."

"No."

"Oh," she said. "But you know a lot about him."

"I do."

"How come?"

"I just do."

"Oh."

We watched for a bit. Then for some reason I told her about how John Leach, Archie's older brother, died as a baby, before Archie was even born. I told her about how his mother suffered from depression, and never got over that baby dying, and how eventually Archie's father had his mother committed to a lunatic asylum, and told his son she'd gone away to get some rest, and then even told him she'd died.

Elizabeth was quiet when I finished. "That's a terrible story," she said.

Neither of us spoke for a time.

Later, she said, "You got any brothers?"

"No," I said. "Kind of. Not really."

"What's that mean?"

"Doesn't matter."

"I don't have any brothers," she said. "Must be nice to kind of have one, anyway."

I didn't answer, and she didn't say any more after that. I regretted telling her that story about Archie Leach's dead brother. Sometimes I don't know why I say the things I say. I guess I was unsettled. Earlier I'd gone in to clean and I thought I'd see her, in her usual spot. I thought she'd be excited about the Bergman double feature. But she wasn't there, and I was sad about that, and angry that I was sad.

I tried to watch but I couldn't pay attention. I moved my foot across the floor so that it was touching Elizabeth's foot. But just barely. She probably didn't even feel it. She probably didn't even know my foot was there, so I thought it was okay.

A WEEK LATER, the raccoons were gone. I went in early to check on them, calling out before I slid the crawl space panel open so I wouldn't scare the mother or the kits. I knew right away they were gone. Not hiding, not sleeping, just gone. You could hear the absence.

I hauled the canisters into the booth for the day's double feature. When I walked in, I found a reel already running. Russell must have come in early, I thought. He was running *Casablanca*, which we were supposed to have shipped back on Friday with the other Bergman films.

From the booth I could look down through the glass into the darkened theater and see the two of them. Side by side in the third row, at the end. Her ribboned head resting on Russell's shoulder, the two of them flickering like movie stills: here, and gone, and here, and gone again.

I let them be.

When the matinees ended and the place was empty, I went out into the late afternoon and slid onto my bike. I rode up and down the banks of the river, and alongside the highway, and through the underpass that ran beneath the spur of the old C&A rail line, long abandoned. I went down every street, riding too fast. People were out, in their yards and in the fields, but I didn't wave, didn't register them. My face was burning. I wasn't thinking of anything. I was fixed on the curve of the road, on the long white bloom of trees along River Street, on the smell of witch hazel and jasmine, on the sound—Connie's sound—of the streetlamps buzzing to life. I drove my legs and made it to the top of Battlement Hill, and when I reached the top, I kept going down the other side, into Delray, around bends and over smaller hills, past the Catholic church and the penny candy store and the high school where I'd be going soon enough, and on into Youngstown, where the asphalt was smooth and the lawns were already green.

I turned off the main road and followed a winding street toward the river, and finally stopped my bike in front of a brick house on a cul-de-sac, tucked between a pair of great weeping willows. It was dark by then and the cul-de-sac's only streetlamp was broken, so I stood in the nightshadows, the same place I'd stood twice before, and looked in on the people who lived there. Another couple was visiting tonight. I saw through the lighted windows a man with a dark beard and a tall woman with her hair in a tight bun, standing side by side in the living room, talking to someone out of the frame.

I waited.

Then she was there. No hair ribbon tonight, just her dark shining hair falling down around her shoulders. Maybe she looked a little older than the version in the theater. Maybe she didn't say *grand* anymore, or maybe she never did, and I only remembered it that way. But she was still a beauty. In her right arm she held a boy, a toddler. I thought he looked like me. I thought maybe he looked like me. But I wasn't sure.

The broken streetlamp above me buzzed and flickered: on, then off again.

She didn't turn. If she had, if she'd seen me in that flicker of light before the scene outside went dark again, she might have thought I was a ghost. Just a ghost from a story she used to know.

In a movie, this moment would matter. You'd be able to tell as you watched that it mattered. Because of the stillness. Because of how everything was framed just so, and how the world fell silent except for the rattling of the wind in the night trees. And you'd remember it was the third time. The story's supposed to change when the third time comes.

I don't know what I thought would happen. I guess I thought I'd say goodbye and somehow be done with it, with her. Then I'd go home and tell Russell, my father, and we'd talk about what it meant. And then we'd leave this place. Or we'd stay. Either way, we'd move on.

But all I did was watch from beneath the broken streetlamp, and sway in the March wind. And though I didn't know why, I said these words in my head, and I kept saying them until she left the window and disappeared into the house to join the others, and the evening rushed in all around me: I'm not gone. I'm not gone. I'm not gone.

Swan Song

BENTLEY THOUGHT THE audition went well. He was nervous, sure, but it made sense that he'd be nervous. More than a decade since his last audition, eight years since his last role. And he just really wanted the part, even though the movie's plot was, well, incomprehensible. The plot was batshit. But it was a nice part—small, but nice. He'd play *the estranged father of Enzo, Luke's best friend.* Luke was the main character, and also imaginary. He was having some kind of existential crisis, which Bentley supposed made sense. Other than that, he had no idea what was going on. The dad, Bentley's character, appeared in only a handful of scenes, including one on the beach at Laguna toward the end. That's the one Bentley liked. A critical scene for young Enzo, Bentley surmised. Only a few lines of dialogue, nothing too dramatic or heavy-handed, just a father and his boy talking. But what there was, was lovely.

"We're thrilled you came in to read." The casting director touched his arm as she walked him out. Just one of those people who needed to make contact. Or maybe she thought he looked as if he needed something more encouraging than a handshake?

"It's a wonderful part." Bentley smiled when he reached the door. "He seems, I mean. His backstory, that is. Such complexity."

She said, "You did well."

Bentley smiled again. He said, "I never had a son."

"We'll be in touch," she said.

He left the audition and walked around the corner, where he sat on a bench outside a frozen yogurt shop, enjoying the afternoon sun before catching the bus back home. He sent Molly a quick text to let her know he'd finished up, and she texted him back immediately: three hearts and a monkey emoji, which meant she was excited. He ate his frozen yogurt and brooded over his line readings. Had he played it too small? With too little nuance? With too much nuance? He wasn't sure that was a thing, too much nuance. And then that weird comment about never having a son.

A boy of four or five walked past with his mother, eyes fixed on the giant ice cream cone in his small hand. The ice cream was already beginning to melt. The two of them made it to their car, and then, while the boy's mother searched her purse for the car keys, he turned his head to look over at Bentley. The ice cream cone was up by his mouth. He blinked a few times at Bentley as if to bring him into focus. Then he froze. Bentley smiled at him. The boy's mouth fell open and the cone tilted in his hand, and Bentley watched as a giant scoop of chocolate ice cream fell to the pavement at his feet. The boy didn't seem to notice. Instead his eyes widened, he drew in an enormous breath, and he began to scream.

When Bentley Boa was four years old, his childhood doctor speculated (flicking cigarette ash at the trash can while Bentley sat across the room a ways, *but clearly within earshot*) that the boy probably had a dozen years in him at best. "Like a dog?" asked Bentley's mother, not trying to be awful, just trying to wrap her head around all of it. With his hunchback, his sloping forehead, his cauliflower ears, his useless clubfoot, and his misshapen nightmare of a nose—on top of the heart problems—Bentley had never been the easiest child to parent. "Exactly like a dog," the doctor said, with maybe too much good cheer.

As a child, Bentley read a lot of books, played solitary games, and daydreamed over the New Jersey summers. His features were frightening enough that he didn't suffer much bullying, which he tried to appreciate. He thought a lot about his soul, and if he had one.

"Of course you do," his mother said. They were in the movie theater watching *Heaven Can Wait*, where heavenly Warren Beatty looked just like earthly Warren Beatty. Same age, same clothes, same exact face. And even when Warren Beatty's character's soul switched bodies with someone else on earth, he still looked exactly like Warren Beatty.

"But what does it *look* like?" Bentley asked. "Will it have a hunchback? And cauliflower ears?"

"Of course not."

"Then how"—Bentley trying to think this through, all of nine years old—"I mean how will you *recognize* me?"

A man behind them leaned forward to shush them both then, which drew a characteristically withering glance from Bentley's mother, who explained that her *goddamn son* had some questions about his *goddamn soul* and that it would be best for everyone ("but mostly you") if the guy just sat his ass back down.

Then she turned to Bentley and said, "You're overthinking it, kid."

Still, it made sense to Bentley that souls would look like the people they'd inhabited. And since he couldn't picture a soul who looked like him, he decided that he probably just didn't have one. He wondered, though, if he shouldn't make an extra effort to be kind, to have a generous heart, just on the off chance that he was wrong.

In high school his mother took them out to Los Angeles for a job. By then his heart problems were being managed well enough, but Bentley—never totally forgetting the doctor's words—gave little thought to what he'd do after graduation, to what kind of life he'd make for himself. When the time came to leave home, he moved from one odd job to another, places where he could be out of sight, or where his appearance could actually be of help: the library, a costume shop, the morgue, the wax museum. It was a coworker at Madame Tussaud's on Hollywood Boulevard who, mortified by Bentley's lack of ambition, dragged him to his first casting call. The audition was in the back room of a warehouse that looked like the scene of a double murder, for the role of Henchman #3 in *Lights Out, Sleepyhead.* Bentley had just bungled the first of his two lines—"This ain't gonna end pretty, Sleepyhead," which Bentley twisted into "Looks like it's not, or I mean it isn't, or ain't, a pretty ending! Sleepyhead!"—when the director held up his hands, apoplectic. "Merciful Christ in heaven," he said, "I've seen enough." Bentley had heard some version of this more than a few times in his life, and had learned the best thing was to glide quietly away, so as to absorb no more than a glancing blow. So he limped toward the door with an apologetic wave. The director stood up so quickly that he knocked over his chair, and told Bentley to stop. Bentley stopped and waited. "Yes?" he said. And the director said, "You are *perfect.*"

Perfect, he meant, for Henchman #2, The Meat Man. Who was on the wrong end of a vat of sulfuric acid (Bentley wondered if there was a right end) way back in *Rise and Shine, Sleepyhead.* The Meat Man had only a few more lines than Henchman #3, and he died horribly at around the forty-five minute mark. But the part was his.

And no one, ever, had called Bentley Boa perfect before.

The film was quickly in and out of theaters. But other filmmakers, eager to round out their stable of villains, took notice. Bentley was cast as a deranged crime boss in *Wicked City*, and then a deranged hit man in *Kill Zone*. That led to a part as a deranged clown in *Welcome to Terror Land* and *Welcome to Terror Land 2: Hellclown*. It was in *Welcome to Terror Land 2* (shortened to just *Hellclown* for the video re-release) that Bentley had his signature moment. It came in the final scene, Hellclown surrounded by National Guardsmen in the center of the Rose Bowl, attack helicopter hovering overhead. Captain Blake Madsen of the LAPD—the same Blake Madsen whose family, not excluding an adorable terrier named Winston, had been eaten by Hellclown back in *Welcome to Terror Land*—gave Bentley's character one last chance to surrender and admit his evil.

Hellclown roars with rage, was the direction in the screenplay. The next scene would find Hellclown obliterated by a missile launcher.

"I'd like to make it kind of, like, poignant," Bentley said to the director, before the shot. "Like it's more of a howl than a roar, almost?"

"It's a roar."

"But maybe a howlish one? I'm thinking, you know, he has all this anguish? I mean yes, obviously he's terrible, there's the murders and the brutalization and the business with Winston but—" The director cut him off and explained how little of a shit he actually gave, just as long as it was a giant motherfucking roar.

So Bentley roared.

The sound began in the pit of his stomach. From there it unfolded outward, expanding in size and ferocity, taking with it—judging by the sound—bits of spleen, lungs, heart, jagged chunks of soul. Officially it lasted fifteen seconds. For the other actors and the crew on set, it seemed much longer. ("Something like a cat, stuffed inside a bag of gravel," said the key grip to a *Variety* reporter, "dragged through an airplane propeller.")

The roles kept coming. Bentley played a deranged, chainsaw-wielding mutant in *Chainsaw Mutants* and *Chainsaw Mutants Take Manhattan*, and had a memorable double role in *Chainsaw Mutants vs. Hellclown*. He took parts as cannibals, as murderous backwoods handymen, as deformed laboratory assistants, as reanimated corpses, as deformed handymen, as reanimated (and usually deformed) cannibals, and as semi-gelatinous blobs of malevolence.

He became, for a while, a celebrity. Theaters began midnight showings of his films, college kids crowding the theaters wearing Styrofoam hunchbacks, ready to scream deliriously whenever Bentley came onscreen. "The Villain We Love to Hate," is how *Rolling Stone* described him for the interview piece, in 1993. For the photograph, they asked him to hold a puppy in one hand and a knife in the other. Bentley was so high on cocaine that, when two months later his agent handed him the magazine, he had no memory of it at all. But he held the puppy over his mouth, and smiled.

His phone buzzed as he rode the bus back to Glendale. A text from David. *Sorry—will call you in a few.* (But why *sorry*?)

He enjoyed riding the bus. Molly thought it was an affectation, and maybe it was. He sat in the back and studied the other passengers. Discreetly, of course. You're okay with George Clooney staring at you on a bus. You're probably kind of *flattered* by George Clooney staring at you. You're looking around for the best lighting to make sure George doesn't see your coffee stain birthmark or the mole on your neck, which might cause him to flinch, or even worse, shudder. Then you'd have to apologize, or at least you'd want to apologize. I'm sorry you had to stare at this mole and I will strive to do better, George. But it's different when it's Hellclown. Even an aging Hellclown.

He was approaching sixty now, and the hump had gone down some. Diminishing bone mass, the doctor said. And his features had, well maybe not softened exactly, but *settled in*. Bentley's mother liked to tell him as a child that someday he would grow into his head. Maybe that's what finally happened. He now looked—almost—like an ordinary old man, or at least he liked to think so. Mol said she was so used to him that everyone else looked funny to her, everyone else looked *weird,* but that was Mol. He wasn't recognized or gawked at as much these days, the occasional screaming kid with an ice cream cone aside, so maybe it was true. Maybe he was just ordinary. Not exactly a great selling point, since no one wanted a supervillain who looked like an ordinary old man with a hump.

Well. Ancient history, anyway.

The Ballad of Luke and Enzo wasn't going to revive his career, he knew that. But still. It would be nice to be remembered for one last, better thing. For something small, but true.

Across the aisle, a gaunt, blank-faced twentysomething began tapping his foot obsessively. Bentley watched him surreptitiously. Baggy, red-rimmed eyes. Flushed face. Clearly there was something going on there. Some storm being weathered. The guy held an unread newspaper in his lap, opened to the Sports section, but turned upside down. In a movie script he'd be one of the early villains. Not the main villain, not a mastermind or a psychopath, but one of the early ones. More of a sub-villain, existing only to serve the hero's development, or to act as a kind of comic relief. He would just be Tapping Guy in the script, because he didn't need a name.

One last role, Bentley thought.

A little dramatic there. Sure. A little *Shakespearean.* The old magician (and what was an actor but a kind of magician?) summoning his powers one last time. Then to be relinquished, forever. *This rough magic I here abjure.* Such words. He'd played Caliban once, up in Mendocino. Four women passed out in the front row when he came out on stage, and another vomited. Not their fault. He'd sat backstage, listening to the actor who played Prospero. Silently mouthing the lines in the shadows. Maybe he'd say that to himself the day they wrapped on *The Ballad of Luke and Enzo* as he walked off set. His *nunc dimittis.* He could even say that to Mol—*it felt like my* nunc dimittis, *Mol.* She wouldn't laugh at him, much.

Tapping Guy was visibly perspiring now, a clear signal, if they'd been on set, that something was going to happen. A clear signal that Tapping Guy was only seconds away from (let's say) standing and making some terrible announcement. Because what other kind of announcement could you make on a bus? There just aren't any good bus announcements. The audience understands that there aren't any bus announcements that leave you thinking *I'm glad I was here for this announcement.* You don't even need to hear the words to know it's going to be terrible.

And then what?

Well. Bentley—Bentley's character, that is—would set down his own, correctly positioned reading material—a John Le Carré novel, maybe, or something ironic like the *Enquirer*—with a kind of exasperated sigh. He'd grumble something cool and laconic under his breath. *God, I hate public transportation.* The reluctant hero. And then—

Then, well, he'd proceed to coolly and mercilessly dispatch this motherfucker. Sure. Later he'd squint through the cigarette smoke as Tapping Guy was tucked into the back seat of a patrol car, while Bentley's captain (his *ex*-captain) reminded him he's a civilian now.

Don't go playing the hero any more, Malone.

Malone. Yes.

But of course no one talked that way. Not really. No one acted that way in the real world. In the real world, the guy on the bus who stands up is only damaged, only broken. Not a supervillain. Not comic relief or comic tension. And everybody, all of them, would suffer for it. Or maybe they wouldn't suffer, maybe they'd survive, but there would be nothing exhilarating about it. There would be nothing about it that wasn't essentially tragic.

Unless Bentley (Bentley's character, or no, this is real life, Bentley *himself*) stood up and, like, talked to him. Wouldn't that be something? Just talked to him like a human being. Maybe he'd never get to play Malone, but he could be *that* guy, couldn't he? The guy who tries to make a connection? He'd stay calm even though he was nervous too—how could he not be nervous?—and he'd speak. And it wouldn't be a one-liner, it wouldn't be a movie quip. Just something true. *Hey, let's talk. Nobody's going to hurt you, son.*

Son. Well.

Bentley's phone buzzed.

"I hope you're outside," David said. "I mean, tell me you're outside. The weather's beautiful, *beautiful*."

"Come on," said Bentley.

"Not to be," said David. It's what he always said when Bentley didn't get a part: *Not to be.* "But she said she really liked you. It just wasn't the right movie, that's the thing."

Bentley was silent. Traffic had picked up and the bus was creeping along. From his seat he could make out a crowd gathering in a park a few blocks down, many of them pointing up at something he couldn't see.

"She loved you, though. Totally loved you. Wasn't you, it was the part. She said to make that crystal clear. Character is supposed to be, you know, this regular guy. But she said she liked you. Must've said it three times."

"She loved me," said Bentley.

"Right. That's what I said."

"Okay," said Bentley.

"Look, I've got to run. Don't sweat this. I'll call you tonight, tomorrow at the latest. Or this weekend."

After hanging up, Bentley stared out the window. It wasn't the end of anything. It felt that way, but it wasn't the end. God, it felt that way.

Another buzz. A text from Mol. *Chicken in fridge looks bad.* Sad face. *Fish or fish tonight?* Monkey emoji.

He thought then of calling her. He wanted to call her. But then he had the thought that, right at this moment, she was still excited for him. Happy with possibility. And he would be taking that away from her by telling her about David's call. Eventually he'd tell her, or maybe he wouldn't have to tell her—he'd walk in the door and she'd see it on his face. She'd say *They don't deserve you.* It would just be something to make him feel better, and they'd both know it, and still it *would* make him feel better.

For now, though, she was excited. He could go a little while longer before telling her. He could do at least that much for her.

The bus was coming up beside the park. Bentley stood and pulled the cord, without having any idea that he was about to do it. Seconds later he was crossing the street toward the park, and looking up with everyone else.

It was a kite festival. Across the sky swam dragons, pterodactyls, swans, swordfish, octopi, teddy bears, galloping horses. The park itself, in the shadow of the menagerie, was crowded with picnic blankets and lawn chairs and dogs and people, people everywhere. He found a spot near a group of picnicking college kids and traced the path of the kites for a while.

An orange and gold dragon swooped down about twenty feet, eyes blazing, before getting caught in an updraft, attack averted. The crowd ooh'd and aah'd.

This was good. This was what he needed. Molly would love this, too. She'd love the sweet, innocent weirdness of it. His breathing slowed. All at once he felt okay again. Maybe this wasn't the end. But if it was, then so be it.

This rough magic I here abjure.

All at once he wanted to go home.

Nearby, someone said, "No fucking way." One of the college kids, a blond with perfectly bronze skin and dope-glassy eyes, had turned to look up at Bentley from the blanket. His friends all turned as well. Four men and two women. Drenched in sunlight, they looked impossibly young, healthy, attractive.

"Bentley *fucking* Boa," said Bronze Guy. He climbed unsteadily to his feet.

Bentley did his best to smile, squinting up at him now. Bronze Guy was a full foot taller. "Ah, hello," he said, and waved to the rest of the group.

"I fucking *knew* it. Fucking Hellclown."

"Bullshit," said one of the others. "That ain't Hellclown." But he stood up too, spilling half his beer. Another giant. A land of giants, it was.

Bentley's phone buzzed. Molly again. "I'm sorry," he said, waving the phone at the group, "but I need to take this."

"Dude," said Bronze Guy. "You were like a fucking *maniac* in that movie."

"So that hump is real, no shit?" asked his friend.

"I've got to take this," Bentley repeated.

"You okay with us touching it?"

"We just want to touch the hump, dude," said Bronze Guy. "For luck, and shit." A drunken giggle followed.

Bentley walked away and answered the call. The wind was picking up. Monstrous shadows darted across the grass around him. "Molly," he said. "I can't hear you at all."

"Bentley mother-fucking Boa," said Bronze Guy. "I mean, *damn.*"

"Jesus, leave him alone already," said one of the women.

"Mol," said Bentley.

"Do the roar for us, man." Followed by: "Fuck, yeah. Do the roar, motherfucker."

"I'm heading home now," Bentley said. "If you can hear me."

"Maybe the guy's an asshole."

"Leave him the fuck *alone.*"

"Freak *and* an asshole."

Bentley hung up. He was breathing hard, with his back still to the group.

"Freak," repeated Bronze Guy, and burped loudly.

"Shit, I'm just gonna touch it."

Someone—Bentley didn't know which one it was—grabbed his hump and squeezed.

Bentley turned, took hold of the one who'd grabbed him by the collar. The guy was taller than Bentley but drunk and off balance, and Bentley threw him easily to the ground. He sat on the guy's chest and knelt on his arms to pin them down. This happened quickly. The others were too stunned, or too drunk, to react immediately. Bentley punched the guy in the side of his face. He'd never thrown a punch before, not in real life, and he marveled that he was able to do it at all. He threw a second punch, and this one landed square in the middle of the guy's nose. This one hurt more—it hurt like hell—but it felt better, too. Honestly it felt pretty good. He punched the guy again in the same place, and felt the nose give way under his fist. Blood sprayed across the guy's face and onto the blue picnic blanket beside his head. Someone started to scream. It was a high-pitched sound, desperate, sort of animalistic, and it was coming from Bentley. It felt good to scream. It felt absolutely fucking wonderful to scream. The guy looked scared now, and Bentley hated him for it. He had never laid a hand on anyone in his fucking life and this guy was scared. He screamed down into the guy's face, he fucking roared, and punched him again. The guy was crying now. Just a kid really. Bentley could see he was just a kid. He wanted to stop then but he couldn't. He just needed to punch the guy one more time. Needed to. One more time would be enough. He hoped that one more time would be enough. So he punched him again, and then two people grabbed him from behind and threw him back onto the grass.

He rolled onto his back and looked up at the sky. A giant octopus swam past, blocking out the sun. Then they started in on him.

MUCH LATER, MOLLY opened the front door. She didn't say anything, only watched him pay the driver and exit the cab. It was getting dark. He'd called her from the hospital and told her what had happened, without going into many details. The boy was okay, he said. The boy was probably okay. She asked him other questions. Yes, he said, I'm fine. Some bruises, he said. Maybe a black eye. No, he didn't want her to come. No, he didn't have more to say. He sounded lost. He sounded young, she thought, or old. Come home, she said.

Now she met him at the door. He looked like a mess and he wouldn't make eye contact with her. She brought him inside, prepared an ice pack for his face, and sat beside him on the couch in the unlighted living room as the night slipped in. He said nothing, but she thought he seemed better. Calmer.

Come with me, she said.

Finally he looked at her. He nodded.

In the bedroom, once they had brushed their teeth side by side, in silence, she closed the curtains and pulled back the covers and turned out the light.

Then they talked. He told her about the audition, about the director's hand on his arm. He told her about the boy's ice cream falling over into the street, about the bus ride and Tapping Guy and Malone. About the call from David. You should have called me then, she said, and he said, I know. She asked him if the sky looked different then, because they'd talked before about how the sky can seem to change sometimes because of something you went through or something you felt. And he said Yes, and he told her about the dragons and octopi above the park. Why octopi, she said, smiling in the dark. He said he didn't know. She asked if there were monkeys and he said he didn't know that, either. And then, she said. So he told her about Bronze Guy, and about wanting to be home all of a sudden, and about everything falling to pieces. Ah baby, she said. You must have been afraid. I'm a monster, he said, and she said, No. She said today wasn't a good day, that's all it was. Tomorrow you will be good. And the world will be good.

And she told him then about her day. About her lunch with Ellen, and about Ellen's joke that she didn't really get—something she'd read in *The New Yorker* or someplace—and Ellen got the punch line all mixed up, but she laughed pretty hard anyway because Ellen never told any jokes, and it just made her happy. Did you get to paint today, he asked, and she said, A little, on the garden scene, the one he liked—the melting garden, he called it, because the colors all ran together like a song or a dream—but she was too distracted. She told him about what she was thinking during his audition (that play in Mendocino, how his eyes shone when he was on stage, and that place where they had dinner right on the water), and the music she was listening to (Etta James, Nina Simone), and how she pictured the audition room (gray, austere, with a fold-out table and a few chairs, and a vase of tulips on the fold-out table, and for some reason a blurry photograph of Orson Welles on the back wall, and he said Yes and yes and yes, and no but maybe he'd only missed the Orson Welles photograph and it was there all along). She told him about how afraid she was when she couldn't reach him after their call was disconnected. About the horrible things she imagined, and the amazing things she imagined to try to counteract the horrible things (that he'd run into an old best friend who had disappeared under mysterious circumstances many years ago, that he'd been stopped on the street and asked to give the President of the United States his autograph, leading to a long bull session about something or other, and he—the President—really wanted to come visit their home and meet this Molly person, too). But she told him she didn't really believe in any of the amazing things. So she left the house to find him. She drove toward Reseda. Along the way she stopped at Sign of the Whale and Frisky Pete's and Moody's and asked the bartenders and everyone at the bar if they'd seen him. She left messages for everyone they knew. She got lost, the way she always got lost. When he called from the hospital she was sitting in a diner parking lot on Van Nuys. There were streaks of red and orange across the western sky and she thought the world might come to an end. She hung up and watched the sun go down. She told him all these things as they lay together in the dark, and more. And a long time later, they fell asleep.

The Long Shadows

I'M WITH ROOK on top of an old three-story building at the edge of the city. Whitebeard says the building was once a factory that manufactured crackers flavored with chicken dust. I don't know how Whitebeard knows this, or what to make of it. I don't remember crackers, or chicken.

Though it's midday, we can see little: the dim forms of tall buildings, the gray blurs of cars moving in every direction, the shadow people who walk below us and who populate the earth. It is a world, I think, ever at dusk. Even sounds are muffled and darkened.

"It is a world," I confide to Rook, "ever at dusk."

Rook flits rudely beside me and makes a primitive phlegmy grunty sound. Whitebeard assigned me as Rook's mentor, and already I think he is not bright. He manifests, for one thing, as only an inky blob. As more of an inky blob than the rest of us. All darkness and teeth and eyes. He swirls in the gray air, shapeless, aggressively stupid.

"Hungry," blurts Rook. Because Rook is a blurter. "Nothing here." There's a streetlamp glowing mutely below us, and Rook darts toward it, moving with the grace of a malevolent moth. He slams against it once, twice, a third time, then returns.

"It's not intelligent to do that," I say. "Do you know what that means? To be not intelligent?"

"*Hungry*," he spits.

"There." I gesture, more or less, at the apartment building across the way.

Rook turns, hisses: "Only gloom." A restless impatient dumb blurting hissing darting blob, Rook.

Still. He's right. Even the rectangles of lighted apartment windows shine little brighter than the surrounding dark. Easier to follow things in motion—cars passing by, shadow people walking and going about their lives, children racing—but they're still only darkness against darkness.

I admit there is much I don't know. I don't know how long I've been here, how long I've been anywhere. I don't know how many of us there are. All I've known is our small group, which hunts and feeds together. If it's called feeding, I don't know. It seems different than what the shadow people do. Maybe scavenging. (*Scavenging*—I don't remember where this came from, rough scratchy word.)

Some things I remember. Whitebeard. His glowing beard taking shape (coalescing, yes) from within the void. His booming voice, beckoning: *Come, there is much to learn.* And then the first feast. Hard to forget. The boy in the ravine, body twisted, eyes glassy and wide, half-frozen in the snow as he slipped away, which dulled him according to the others, but even so. The tastes, sounds, colors! The *somethingness* of it all. And then the long Great Learning, why it matters, what we do. The Cosmic Circle, as Whitebeard calls it. (When he said this, I imagined the word "cosmic" crackling like a lightning bolt, white blue jagged beautiful glowy word, and missed some of the rest.)

And of course learning how to find our next meal.

Rook is of course at the beginning of the Great Learning, and knows almost nothing. He has no faith. He doesn't know, as I do, about the woman in Apartment 4F. I watched from this roof as she was wheeled in by the others on a thing, a roller-bed thing, could see the way she, in her roller-bed thing, glowed suddenly brighter and with more color than the surrounding world. Her soulstuff beginning to surface, silver-blue. That was three days ago. Since then I have monitored from here on the rooftop, waiting for the light to bloom.

"It is faint," I agree. "But it's there. Fourth floor. Sixth from the corner."

Rook shifts, turns, agitates. "Not there. Hungry. *Hungry. Hungry! Nothing!*"

I suggest gently that he look with his heart. "With your mind's heart. With your mind's secret heart."

Rook croaks, spins like a profoundly stupid being, spits. "Means nothing."

"Whitebeard says it." Though privately I agree with Rook.

"You call him that," Rook says. "Why? Shouldn't."

"You shouldn't be a dumb-dumb," I say. Which shuts him up for a moment, so we both watch in silence. But again, he's right. Whitebeard isn't

Whitebeard's name. He may not be, probably is not (was not?) a he. Like the rest of us he is mostly formless, neither smoke nor solid. He looks to me like a walrus, on the blobby side and with what appear to be flippers, but with a luminous and undulating white beard. I named him as I've named the others, though names are *verboten*. Horseman for example is called Horseman because he makes a terrible whinnying sound sometimes, and because the one I called Luna claimed that his form resembled a seahorse. We nodded when she said this, and pretended we knew or remembered seahorses. "Watch," she said, and we gathered darkly around her on the rooftop, all except Whitebeard, as she showed us the memory of a seahorse she had stolen for herself. It shone brightly at the center of our circle, blue-green and lovely and twisting in the lesser shadows. Its spiny tail furling and unfurling. Then she snatched it away so we couldn't take it for ourselves. She liked all things green and fluttering and strange. I named her for her favorite, the luna moth. And for the moon, because she was always there above me when I looked for her. She's gone now.

"There," says Rook.

"Told you." Though I don't see a thing. Apartment 4F stays dark.

But Rook is up, already starting the call for the others when I see it—not in 4F but two floors down, on the corner. The room behind the window is softly aglow. Rook tries to signal the way he's been taught but his voice is warbling and unpracticed. I rise over the street and amplify the sound, a fluttering wail like a loon over a frozen lake. (I remember loons.) Even as I call, Rook is diving toward the bloom of light, and I follow. We swoop through the dusk and dart in through the window pane.

The scene inside is blinding.

There are four of them. Two smaller ones, lying in the corner of the room where they've fallen. Two others close by, older and bigger, one atop the other. Blood and smoke and a gathering death-hum in the air. I tell Rook to take the little ones and I move to the larger pair, crumpled together on the floor. The others will come soon—there's plenty for all of us here—but there's no time to waste. The ghost of a siren sounds, far off, growing closer. The bodies pulse with light and color, as if they're about to burst. I take a breath—I don't really take a breath, but I imagine taking a breath—and plunge my smoky claws into the closest body. Reverently. In what I imagine is a reverent way. Whitebeard said we should be reverent. I clutch the soulstuff and tear it free, opening my mouth wide as the ribbons unfurl, some burning brighter than others—

hot afternoon baking in the sun on the beach with Mandy (Mandy hello I live next door I saw you moved in and oh she was such a sad kid but why) side by side going downhill TOUCHING FINGERTIPS (I wish I asked her why poor kid but I loved her and later she died I should've gone to the funeral I never even called I'm sorry Mandy) high school first to graduate proud so proud mama EVERYTHING IN SILVER AND BLUE, Mischa, Dee, Bey (that pretty hair) in the dark of a theater showing something too fast violent but whatever it's nice to be next to him (Mookie such a dumb name groping motherfucker but oh I didn't know shit and he didn't either) Bey with her little boy first COO SO SWEET and why ain't you happy (damn Bey get loose of this shit) holiday road trip not a road trip an escape no no a liberation fuck Newark we're lighting out for the territories bitch maybe just one hit but we shouldn't really shouldn't (just want to be happy for a fuckin' minute).

The moments crowd past as the life rushes out of her without sequence or pattern. I swallow it all in great gasping mouthfuls, Mandy and Mischa and Dee and Bey and Mookie, delicious terrible life unspooling like smoky bitter candy, and it makes me tremble. I'm still trembling when new tastes announce themselves, new sounds, ribbons of darker color as the other one's soulstuff emerges full force, merges with the last of hers, all fury and incoherence at first, then the rest of it coming loose, embers rising from a fire

playground fights and talking-to's and almost-whippings (run like hell she used to say run like hell boy) a small plastic dome blue on the bottom kids ice skating on a frozen lake, pine trees and a little log cabin with a post a light post a light pole a lamp pole a LAMP POST yes, silver and white SNOW FALLING when you shook it (snow globe that's what it was called that was mine that was what he left me when he left) sunlight glinting off the hoods of old Thunderbirds and Mustangs and the air so thick and humid we can feel ourselves breathe it in when we laugh because no one can find us (me and Ko and Ko's little brother who went out to Oakland later on and got shot to death because of some stupid shit) in the blocks ready to go can see my breath in the air muscles coiled like a jaguar ha but it's true and nothing matters nobody matters and maybe he's in the stands somewhere ha maybe he's watching his boy (Where'd you go anyway motherfucker) hips moving who's that with Bey with the smile damn. And more and more—too much for me alone, but I swallow what I can. Only the snow globe I keep aside. And the memory of these words: lamp post (not a streetlight but a *lamp post*) and jaguar. I don't know this jaguar, but it moves like a dark diamond through my mind.

The muted wail of sirens grows louder outside. Someone pounds on the door and I break free as the others arrive through the window at last to take up what's left. Rook, on the other side of the room, is a tornado of shadow and teeth. Zero dignity or restraint. Savoring nothing.

Later Rook finds me, back on the roof. I hide the globe in my smoky folds.

"Why you save things," he says. "Just eat. *Eat eat eat*." Drifting closer as he speaks, maw clattering, full of hunger.

I drop from the roof and fly. Away from him. Away from the city and toward the moon rising through the clouds on the eastern horizon. The wind sinks its teeth into me. Or no, it does not. But I wish it would. I soar above the tree line, now and then swooping close to the ground as I cross backyards and outbuildings, ballparks, abandoned playgrounds and empty parking lots. It's hard to navigate down so low, easy to collide with all I cannot see in the murkiness closer to the ground. But I like being here, so close to the smells and sounds of living things.

Sometime later I come to rest, bobbing gently, beside a thicket of bushes at the bottom of a hill. In the thicket there's a dead spot, a softly glowing hollow, and inside the hollow are my treasures. Baseball cards and pocket watches, stuffed animals and rubber snakes, shark tooth necklaces, wedding rings. And books. Things that meant something to someone else, enough to be held close until the life spilled out of them at the very end. They alone glow in this midnight land like bejeweled ghosts.

At the top of the hill sits a lone white house. A light burns grayly in an upstairs window. I withdraw the globe and inspect it, and look back toward the window, and back at the globe.

Lamp post. The phrase settles into my mind's secret heart.

I don't know why we save things. I don't know why I suggest it to the others, or why they listen. I don't know why it feels the way it feels when I go over my treasure, when I tell stories about it. I think it hurts but I cannot say for sure.

A woman, the slender gray-haired woman who lives in the house on the hill, moves to the back window of the house. She looks out at the field where I am standing-floating, looking back in at her. As if. But no. I imagine she is Luna. Waiting for me to return at the end of a long day of hunting for our food things in the city. Hoping wanting for me. Upstairs our babygirl (Bey, or Mischa) is asleep, with the goodboy Mookie snoring at the foot of the bed, protecting her, protecting us all.

The wind blows through me and sweeps across the field, which is aglow in the light of the rising moon. Up in the house, at the window, my Luna shivers and crosses her arms to her shoulders.

"Horseman," I say, "was born in the bottom of the ocean, and raised by a family of benevolent Horses of the Sea."

All of us but Whitebeard are gathered on the sloped roof of what Luna called an "amputheater," because (she said) the walls had all been cut off, leaving only a stage. It's in the middle of a park in the city. Hundreds of the shadow people are scattered on the grass around the amputheater, listening to the ones on stage who beat things with sticks and scream nonsense. We don't understand the words but the sounds are appealing. We hear the low tones better than the high tones. Sometimes we press our faces down against the roof to feel the noisy thrum vibrate through our souls. Though Whitebeard says we have no souls.

"How?" asks Worm. Worm is a slash of black horror, ten feet tall and no more than six inches wide, with an even thinner stalk extending from the top featuring a single, freakish blue-gray eye. "How he breathed under the water?" We have been present at drownings, have felt and seen the gasping panic of those last moments.

I pause before speaking, to be sure Worm senses my disappointment. "Horseman," I reveal at last, "once had gills. Like fish."

Horseman whinnies, pleased.

"What's benevolent?" whispers Kitty Boo Boo, who named herself.

"Kind," says Worm, thoughtfully. He dips his eye stalk down at us, ignorant of his grossness. "Not trample-stomped him under horse feet. Like could have."

"Hooves," I say. "But yes."

Rook drifts over, hisses, "*Dummies.*" Then he darts away from us to look out over the roof's edge at the shadow people.

I tell the rest about Horseman's rescue by the noble seahorses. About how when he was old enough and had lost his gills, he was sent on his way to be among his true people. There, I say, he had many adventures.

"Horseman robbed banks?" says Horseman. Long ago we witnessed a bank robbery that thrilled us and gave us much to eat.

"No," I say. I have to think quickly, because in fact Horseman's story was going to heavily feature a bank robbery.

"Did he," asks Kitty Boo Boo, "find love?" It's almost all she asks, though she knows nothing of love.

"You know nothing of love," I say.

She turns away in a cloud of smoke, chastened.

I speak instead of Horseman's rise among the shadow people. How he talked little and had modest ambitions, and was perhaps dull, but came to be loved for his great kindness, for the soft and worn baseball glove he carried with him always, for his skill in making crackers flavored with chicken dust, for his—

"Teapots," says Horseman. "Tell." He brings forth one of his teapots, white with blue flowers. We watch it spin slowly in the air before him, and then he snatches it away.

"And for his weird collection of teapots," I say. "But did I say loved by all? No, not all. There was one who challenged him. His lost brother. Who was named—" I glance around to be sure they are listening—"*Thunderbird*."

"Not real," screeches Rook, eavesdropping from the roof's edge. "Lies, stupid."

"You're stupid," I say.

"*You're* not real," says Worm.

Horseman whinnies, impatient. "Tell, tell," he says.

"Was he evil?" asks Worm. "Thunderbird?"

"Did he love?" asks Kitty Boo Boo.

"He was separated from Horseman at birth," I say, ignoring them. "And banished. Exiled to . . . the kingdom of Oak Land." They are silent, dumb, ignorant of this place. "For many moons he did not know the truth of his origin. One day he was out in the great oak forests of Oak Land, and he came across the glorious *jaguar* of legend. A beast so sleek, so wise, so strong, so beautiful, that it drove anyone mad who happened to see it." They are unmoved by this. Cannot fathom a beauty that drives one mad. Cannot, probably, fathom *madness*. I almost say this—*I know you cannot fathom any of this*—but they won't know this word, *fathom*. I heard Whitebeard say it, and demanded he explain it, and now it is a word only the two of us share. So instead I improvise and add that as everyone knows the jaguar also has more than a thousand razor-sharp teeth—

"Beautiful razor-sharp teeth?" asks Kitty Boo Boo, doubtfully.

"What Horseman do?" demands Horseman. "Enough Thunderbird, enough!"

"Sounds make believed," says Worm. "Think maybe you not even know what jaguar is."

Rook laughs and darts around us. Monstrous idiot.

"And you do?" I'm furious now. "Tell your own stories!" And I fling myself from the rooftop.

The rest of the evening I spend in an overgrown graveyard filled with mismatched stones, far outside the city. Not a place for our kind. There's nothing here for us, nothing on which to feed. It seems to me a useless place—a place for those who need no place of their own. But the shadow people come anyway to visit. They commune, they remember things. I can feel them remembering things. So I watch, I listen, in the hope that I'll find something to steal. Now and then I flutter near the brightest of the lighted poles, the *lamp posts*, that line the path through the graveyard. I don't beat against it like a gibbering moron, like Rook. But I do whisper *lamp post,* each time I pass by.

In the morning it's cool and a light rain falls. I wish there was fog, because I like the word and I like the look of the thing the word means. I like the way it sometimes creeps along the ground, hiding and revealing the stones left to mark the dead. I like the way it obscures the world for the shadow people the way ours is obscured. But there is no fog. Only rain. Yet the graveyard isn't empty. An old man, frail and bald and almost as skinny as Worm, stands before one of the more modest stones. He wears a hat that I like, and leans on a walking stick, head bowed. I move closer. I can't read the markings on the stone, but many names are inscribed there. A family of names.

I wait. Hoping he might say something to his dead. That he might give me something. A name, a place, a wound to savor and spin into gold.

He remains silent and motionless. Around us, the city bends, twists into wakefulness, resurrects itself from sleep. The old one bends down to pull weeds from the ground in front of the stone, smooths the dirt there. Then he stands and brushes off his pants. I think that, now, he will depart. Instead he turns his head in my direction. The brim of the hat covers his eyes.

"Leave this place," he says. "You are not welcome here."

I rise quickly and fly into the morning.

~

Whitebeard finds me in the afterdawn, alighting beside me on the roof of a crumbling barn not far from the graveyard. Cows and sheep make noisy awful hopeless sounds around us. I would like to know the name for this sound.

"Speak with me," says Whitebeard. He glides ghost-like from one side of the roof to the other, and I follow, ghost-like myself. Ghost. I wonder if we might say we ghost across the roof. We are not ghosts—we are probably not ghosts—but I like this word. This usage. I tuck it away.

"You are distracted," says Whitebeard.

"The cows, the sheep." I wave a gaseous claw. "The noises they make. Ugh."

"Yes," he says, "it's awful."

"*What* is awful?" I ask.

"The bleating," he says.

Delight. I tuck that away: *the bleating.* Yes. Because it sounds like that, not a groaning or a screaming or a snarling or a grunting but a bleating.

"Nothing else is wrong, then," he says. "Ever since. . . ." He trails off. I know what he wants to say but he can't, not without naming her.

I pause, and then: "Whitebeard."

"Do not call me Whitebeard," he says.

"Of course. Something I thought about today. When I was talking with Horseman—"

"Do not call him Horseman," he says.

"Don't call *who* Horseman?" I ask.

"Horseman," he says. Because Whitebeard may be many things, but humorous is not one of these things. "And the rest. You think I don't know you've given them all names."

"It's just," I explain, "a convenience."

"I had hopes for you," he says. He falls silent then. His beard rises and falls in the gloaming. I admire it, his beard. It is pointless and wonderful. And I admire, too, the word *gloaming,* which I have just now summoned from the black depths, and the word *pointless.* I admire most how they combine together.

"Someone must be responsible," he says. "For the others."

"Well, that's why we have you." Thinking perhaps he is losing it. Come to think of it, he is looking a little frayed. A little undefined around the edges.

"When I'm gone," he clarifies.

"Gone," I repeat.

"I mean not *gone*. Not gone gone."

I study him carefully. "Because you *said* we don't ever die."

"Well. I mean *yes*. The word *die*, you know."

I say nothing to this.

Whitebeard flutters. His beard twists and untwists. "We're not like—them. We don't have these things."

"What *things?*"

"Histories."

"Ah."

"They're *burdens*. Not gifts."

"I mean," I say, "obviously." I do not know this word, *burden*. A not-gift. A thing you give that no one wants.

"It's why we do what we do. We—we unburden."

"Sure," I say.

"You understand, then?"

"Do I *seem* like I understand?" I ask him.

He looks away without answering. "You should be kinder," he says, vaguely. "Especially to Rook."

"Rook is a slobbering nightmare clown. He can barely speak."

"Even so," says Whitebeard. I think he'll say more, then, that he wants to say more, but instead he only repeats: "Even so."

I keep to myself the rest of the day.

In the evening I return to the rooftop where I watched, with Rook, the apartment building across the street. There is no change with the woman in 4F, though I know she is dying. A younger woman comes to visit. She stays for only a short time. It feels obligatory to me. This word, *obligatory*, I don't know. But I saved it once and I think this is what it means. For someone to come without wanting to come. To say goodbye without actually saying goodbye. And then the young woman is gone. She is relieved to have finished this obligatory thing she has done. She hopes, not unkindly, that the old woman dies.

I descend and settle into the back bedroom of apartment 4F. In the other room another young woman waits, reading a book. She isn't family, isn't one of this woman's people, but she is here for this purpose, I understand. To see her through to the end.

I move beside the old shadow woman, look down on her in her roller bed. I think about how I would like to take her hand. Just this once. To be *with.* Not merely *around* or *above.*

Her breath comes now in quiet rasps. She is thinking, dreaming, about what I do not know. But I know she is elsewhere. Immersed in the life that will soon be freed, and upon which I will feed. I wish I could see her clearly, that she was more than paleness and shade. I would like to study the deep lines that life has etched in her face. I would like to see and feel the shape of the thin, bony fingers now curled against the bedsheets. What might that feel like, to take her hand? I watch the rise and fall of her tiny chest. Light blooms around her. She is close. I know she is close.

I stare at my smoky claw, as if to will it into the shape of a hand.

She draws a deep, rattling breath.

The shadow woman in the other room doesn't hear. I'm glad. I don't want her here. What does she know of the old one? What does she know of death? What could she tell the old one to help ease the passage? She is as useless as the young one who came earlier in the day, for her obligatory visit. Let the dying one be alone. Let her move across this boundary alone, with no one but me to see her through, and strip away what binds her.

A fluttering at the window.

Kitty Boo Boo. She settles in across the woman's roller bed from me, looking down at her.

"Maybe it's better," she says, after some time. "To die. To be able to die."

"Go away," I tell her.

"I envy her."

"That's because," I say, "you've always been stupid."

"Now," she says, leaning down. "It is happening."

Frannie is her name, *my love, my sweet Frannie, sweet baby Frannie—*

gulls crying overhead and the sky is blue and there's a face a face I know (forgot how young she was how lovely oh momma) so sad all the time but why when you were loved I wish I knew (but oh she's smiling now and looks so light so untouched she did love me so) running with Maggie being chased down Moffit's Hill as the SUN GOES DOWN but not really chased by who by James brother James gentle James (he doesn't like Jimmy was his dad's name) new to this place Ken-tucky but not alone not anymore and thank you for that (hope you lived long Maggie hope you had adventures James hope you stayed gentle hope you were both loved please have been loved) the dark clouds and the TREES SHAKING in the August afternoon and it should feel this way when someone dies (Aunt Kay who scared me because of the mole but found out she was brilliant and traveled everywhere even to Antarctica) Becca's face can't tell if she's mad don't be mad I take it back unless unless (yes) please (yes) kiss me (yes) PORCHLIGHT FLICKERING ON are you girls ready to come back inside no we're fine we'll stay out here forever thank you thank you.

There's nothing very interesting there, nothing to save, but it is rich and there is so much to eat—

I notice Kitty Boo Boo and stop. She isn't feeding. She's making some sound I've never heard from her or from any of us, a purring gnashing crunching sound that grows and more horrible with each passing second. I understand that she is crying. She is trying to cry and it's awful. And she's eating nothing. Instead, she is gathering all she can into her folds, all the while making the awful crunching sound.

"Stop it!" I snap. "We're missing too much." I snatch at the ribbons and plunge all I can grab into my hideous maw.

"It doesn't matter," says Kitty Boo Boo.

"Dumb-dumb!" I shriek. "It's the *only* thing that matters."

"Why?"

"Because it is! Because—" Everything is going wrong. The life streams out of Frannie faster now, the ribbons stretching and fading as they extend farther and farther from her body.

I say: "Because it's all gone forever without us."

She roars, then leaps through the window and into the dark.

I am frozen, unsure. I could call for the others to help. That is the protocol. Otherwise much will be lost. Which will be terrible, because. Because! I don't know why. I've never known why. I should have asked Whitebeard to explain. To repeat what he had explained when I wasn't paying close attention.

Frannie is almost gone now. Almost emptied. The ribbons are disintegrating, leaving a room of rising ash. I move closer and lower my face to hers. Not to devour or to steal, just to know. The memories are not coherent now, just bubbles of light in the darkness, there and gone in an instant. In the bubbles I see faces, doors, sand, shoes, subway cars, more faces, dolls, gravestones, hands, lips, motorcycles, pineapples, fishing boats, more faces, wheelchairs, airplanes, hopscotch games, roller coasters, pigtails, hamsters, willow trees, train stations, stuffed animals, and still more faces, endless faces, teachers and grandparents and Mother and Father and brothers and friends and bosses and nurses and beggars and drunkards and salesmen and lovers and funeral directors and strangers and children and grandchildren and as each one appears and then disappears forever, Frannie calls out thank you thank you goodbye, and then it all goes dark.

I search through the gray midnightlands for Kitty Boo Boo.

Before dawn I find her at last in the clearing beside a stand of oaks near a school. She has torn herself to pieces. Shredded black flaps lie everywhere in the clearing. But even as I watch, the flaps are reassembling themselves. The process takes some time. I hover nearby until she is whole again. By then the day has risen and the first of the shadow children are arriving for school.

"Come," I tell her. "You must be hungry now. We will find something."

"I'm finished," she says, moving into the shadows of the oaks.

Coming closer, I see that all around her are scattered treasures. Well, "treasures." I count several hundred pairs of multicolored doll eyes, but not the dolls themselves. It seems creepy and useless to me.

"I will eat no more," she says. "Eventually I will die." She adds, quietly: "I must."

"You're talking like a baby. Like a—like a dumb-dumb baby." Which is, okay, not my best. But my hope is to start a fight. I don't know why.

Kitty Boo Boo says nothing.

More shadow children arrive. Their noisy restless energy puts me on edge. A girl with pigtails (but how did I, when did I learn) walks right through us in the clearing on her way to the school. She shivers as she goes past.

"Kitty," I say.

"Leave me." Her voice is not angry. Her voice is not anything. The silence rushes in around us, swallowing us both. I should be glad for the silence. I have always hated her voice. The soft pleading, the endless questions about love. The. Stupid. Endless. Questions. I'm glad it's gone, defeated.

But I don't feel glad. I spin around, agitated. I fly to the treetops and back again. I beat my wings against the trunks.

I dart toward her and ask, hovering, "You want death?"

"I want nothing," she says.

"Follow me."

I take off without looking back, trusting that she's behind me. I feel stupid and furious now. And afraid. Why afraid? Why stupid? Why feelings?

I lead us far beyond the city. For hours we fly, beyond the smaller towns with their slow, quiet lives and their quiet deaths, beyond the churches where they gather to worship their ghosts, past the endless and pointless cemeteries, over countless hospitals where we sense the approach of death and life together, only rooms apart. Here a young man dies on a bloody table after an automobile crash, here a baby comes screaming and bloody into the world, here an old one silently blinks out his final hours alone, here a sweating woman cries out as another baby emerges full of terrified joy. The day bleeds into the night again but we keep flying, until at last the habitations die away and the hospitals and graveyards disappear and the land is silent and dark below us. I feel Kitty Boo Boo beside me, unquestioning.

Eventually something comes visible in the distance. A reddish orange glow on the horizon, small at first, then growing as we approach, until at last it spans the whole length of the horizon in front of us. A curtain of fire twenty feet high, constantly shifting, revealing and concealing some greater darkness just beyond.

I bring us closer, close enough to feel its heat, and then I stop.

"The Hellmouth," whispers Kitty Boo Boo, alighting beside me. "Where Luna went."

"Is this what you want?" I ask. "Then go ahead! I'll watch you. I'll watch you and laugh at how stupid you are. To give everything up."

"Why won't you speak of her?" she asks.

"Because there's nothing to speak of!" I shriek.

She is silent, but doesn't cower from me. Instead she regards me as if she's figuring something out, which I try to ignore. Then she looks toward the Hellmouth. "I see," she says. "I think I see."

"Ha!" I'm shimmering with rage now. "You don't *see* anything! You don't *know* anything! You don't—you are not *Luna*."

The name hangs in the air between us for a moment, silencing us both.

"I know," she says. Then, quietly, she adds, "I'm not going through there."

I roll my eyes. I try to do what I imagine is a rolling of my eyes. "You make sense at last," I say.

"But someday I will," she says.

I refuse to acknowledge this.

"Someday you will too," she says.

This is too much. This is insanity. I unleash a howl so loud and terrible that bits of smoky viscera dislodge themselves from my throat and scatter in the dark fiery air, forcing Kitty Boo Boo to turn away.

Then I fly. Not simply away but up, up, toward the moon that floats grinning and stupid above the black hills of the earth. The moon, the horrible moon, the ridiculous moon that I can never, ever reach. The air thins and darkens around me as I ascend. Through wispy clouds I rise, into the star-black cold of the night sky, and I want to keep rising forever until everything is gone beneath me.

Instead I grow tired, and weak, and I fall. Down through the silent skies toward the gray earth. I make no move to slow my descent, though I know I will suffer when I hit the ground and am smashed to pieces. Eventually I'll reassemble myself. I'll be okay again. I always am.

ONE DAY LONG ago, Luna was simply there with us, arriving from elsewhere. That's where she said she came from, Elsewhere, and my heart soared at this word that I didn't know, but felt. She was small but had great wings that shimmered restlessly, and because she had wings, or something like wings, she alone looked like she belonged in the air above the earth. From the start I was drawn to her, and she to me.

Yes, she to me.

We hunted and fed together, and flew from place to place together, and huddled together on the rooftops, and howled together, and chased each other through the graveyard fog. I was always by her side, and she always by mine, and it seemed as if—somehow—it had always been this way, and could never have been different. Even when we were supposed to be with the others, we stole away. We hid from them. I don't know why or how we came to know each other this way, but we did. It was stronger than hunger, and it was the same as hunger.

"Because we knew each other once," she said, early on.

I asked what she meant, but she didn't answer, instead twirling and beating her wings in the sky above me, full of dark merry joy. And she laughed—she was the only one among us who could laugh, who knew the trick of it, and knew when to do it.

"You are mad," I called up. Because of course I knew what she meant. She meant that we were once like them, like the shadow people.

She sang down to me: "We are their echoes on the earth."

I didn't try to stop her. I knew it was wrong. I knew *she* was wrong, but I wanted to believe, despite what Whitebeard said. And when we were together, there were moments when I did believe. I believed we had these things that Whitebeard said we didn't have: histories. Stories about us that were true, and not just the things we found in books.

It was Luna who loved books. The memories of books. She saved them the way Horseman saved his teapots and Kitty Boo Boo saved her doll eyes, because she loved the way they felt in your hand (she said—as if remembering the time when we had books, and hands to read them with), the way the pages darkened along the edge as you made your way through, the places where you marked your stopping point for the night (*dog ears*, Luna called them, but why). The books she saved had brightly colored covers and well-remembered titles, and were stuffed with pages that were mostly blank except for opening sentences, scattered lines from poems, closing passages, phrases and scraps of dialogue: these clues left for us to decipher. We read them together, over and over, and so we knew these things: that there was no possibility of taking a walk that day, and all happy families were the same, and there was a firing squad and the discovery of ice, and he was to be called Ishmael, and the clocks were striking thirteen on some April day, and 124 was spiteful, and Mother died today, and she would buy the flowers herself, and the snowballs had flung their arcs, and someone was a shadow (but how) of a bird killed by a windowpane. We didn't know the rest. But we knew how the rememberers felt about what they remembered, and what they kept with them to the end. We knew where they were when they finished the books they cherished, what music played as they turned the last pages, how the sky was streaked with purple and orange when they looked up to see how late it was, how their hearts swelled to find the lovers reunited or the lost son find his way home at last, how they fell asleep with the story in their heads to let it continue running. All these things Luna loved, and so I loved them too.

We invented our own stories to please each other. Hers were always better. She gathered threads and wove them, and always surprised. I added big noisy obvious things—bank robberies and invading armies, explosions and car chases, poisoned kings and superheroes. She gave the bank robbers names, and scars, and childhood friends, and she invented scars for the childhood friends, and she fashioned for the poisoned king a favorite stuffed animal, named for a beloved aunt he lost as a boy, and she gave the beloved aunt a story too. Every story sprouted other stories, and each story held within it the echoes of the ones that came before. I couldn't keep it all in my head but she said it didn't matter, it didn't matter as long as we kept it going for as long as we could.

It was Luna, too, who found the house on the hill. There was no death there, no reason to bring us close, but she saw the couple who lived there one day, she said, when she was flying over. Running around in their yard. Chasing each other, laughing. Like us, she said. They are like us. I didn't know what she meant but I agreed.

We watched from outside the window. Luna liked to be there, she said, at the end of day when they were making dinner. To see how they walked around the kitchen, how they talked, picking things up, stirring things, putting things inside of other things, eating and drinking other things all the while—we didn't understand but Luna loved these little details, and made up dialogues for us to explain them. *Darling I need these blobbies cut in two and the insides scooped out,* she'd say, and I'd say *Of course, you know I love the blobbies, but I forgot where my chop board is,* and she'd say *In the hideaway where we keep the food mittens,* and I'd say *Sorry about that, what a dumb-dumb I am sometimes!* And she'd laugh her dark twinkling laugh and say *It's okay and I love you anyway, and get me some of the golden bubble juice in a nice glass pretty please.* And we'd keep going like that until they went to bed. Sometimes we watched them there, too, hovering cloudlike outside the upstairs window. We knew of sex but had never watched it ourselves until then, never had a reason to watch it. It perplexed me. The breathing, the grunting, the sighing. But Luna loved to watch, and eventually she made us try to do the things we saw them do. We lay together in the lot behind the old cemetery, my form levitating above hers, and she sighed and purred and said *Oh God oh God oh God* and I didn't understand that either. But I was happy because she was happy.

Time passed. The shadow couple had a baby, and then sometime later had another. We watched them, too. The house seemed all chaos and lunacy to me, then, and I thought Luna would lose interest, but she didn't. We returned each day and watched their strange, dull, noisy lives play out. Eventually the children grew and left, and the couple was alone together more, which I liked because Luna had said they were like us, and I liked us being alone together. Then one day he was taken away, in one of the roller beds. We could tell he wasn't dying, not then, but he never returned. The children, now grown, returned for a while, and they sat together and talked and ate things and walked the hills together. But then she, the woman, was left alone. And she seemed to do nothing at all, sometimes for hours at a time. Once we followed her to a graveyard, where she stood before one of the stones and read from a book we couldn't see. Then she set the book down by the stone (but why), and returned home to the dark quiet house on the hill.

It was around then, around the time we saw her pointlessly leave the book in the graveyard, that Luna began acting strange. Agitated and uninterested in stories, in hiding from the others, in chasing each other around the graveyard in the fog.

"You're bored with me," I said to her, once. "You don't even laugh now."

"You don't understand," she said.

"I understand a lot," I said. Though I didn't understand. I didn't understand why she kept going back to the house even though there was nothing now to see. There was no couple there like us anymore. There was just a woman growing old alone.

"She spent the whole day writing letters," Luna reported, after an entire afternoon by herself at the house. "She only took a break to lie on the floor with the dog. She hasn't eaten in two days."

"*You* haven't eaten in days," I said.

"You don't understand," she said again.

"What's there to understand?" I demanded.

"The story ended," she said.

"We'll find more stories," I said. "Fun stories. We'll—we'll travel. You said you liked waterfalls. We'll find the biggest one ever! We'll pretend we're going over the falls—on a raft—and we're being chased by bears—with guns—and there's fog and mist and—"

"She's suffering," said Luna.

"Okay," I said. "And yet—fun. Adventure. Waterfalls." I held out to her a glowing miniature waterfall, water crashing into an ice-blue mist, encircled by a dozen blue-green fluttering Luna moths. I'd been saving it for a quiet night under the moon after pretending to smash our bodies against each other, but now seemed like a good time.

She ignored me. "She suffers," she went on, "because it ended. But they both knew it would end."

"I guess," I said. "It always ends. For all of them."

"Exactly!" she cried. "Why set out the way they did, knowing they would suffer? Why become like they became? Why get—tangled—in each other?"

"Who cares?" I said. Exasperated.

"Because it's the answer."

"WHAT IS THE QUESTION?"

She flew off and disappeared. For days she stayed away, and I snapped at the others and told dreadful stories and pretended not to worry. When she returned, many days later, she told me to follow her, and that's when she showed me the Hellmouth.

"This is where you've been spending your time," I said. "This—place?" Of course I knew of it. We all knew it was there. But none of us were foolish enough to go near it.

"You asked," she said. She gestured toward the Hellmouth. "You wanted to know the question."

"I changed my mind. I just—I miss who we were."

"I miss who we never were," she said.

And with that she flew closer to the edge and higher, above the curtain, so she was positioned almost above the mouth itself.

"Stop!" I pleaded. "What craziness is this? What stupidness? Do you want to disappear?"

"I want what they had."

"They had nothing!" I buzzed toward her, flew—accidentally—above the curtain myself. I looked down into the mouth and regretted it. Beneath the curtain of fire, the walls of the Hellmouth swirled and churned, filled with what looked like dust clouds and lightning and shooting stars, blinding bright below the rim before growing darker, infinitely darker, as it went down. The deepest part of it was so black that I thought it must have no bottom. I fluttered away to safety, resisting the urge to pull Luna with me. "Nothing!" I repeated. "They—all of them—get one story. Just one! Dumb! Our stories are endless!"

She looked at me then, and seemed to change. For an instant she was full of color—a glorious blue-green, glowing as bright as the moon itself. Then like a shade pulled down over a vision never meant to be seen, she went dark again.

"Don't be afraid," she said. "I left something for you."

Then she flew across the rim of the Hellmouth, and vanished.

~

I'm with Kitty Boo Boo again, by the house on the hill. Inside, the woman has guests over for a party of some kind. She is sad but laughing, sad but listening, sad but telling stories. It is strange.

"What is it?" she asks. "What did she leave for you?"

I lead her down to the hollow, my secret hollow, where I withdraw a book with an empty blue-green cover. The pages inside are blank except for one, at the end. There, Luna had written, scrawled in some strange hand (but how), a single line in the middle of the page.

WHAT MAKES THE STORY BEAUTIFUL IS THAT IT ENDS

~

When we rejoin the others on the rooftop, Horseman is telling stories. Trying to tell stories. His stories are terrible and too often feature teapots, but I keep my thoughts to myself. Kitty Boo Boo hovers near me but says little.

After we feed—even Kitty Boo Boo feeds—we go back to the roof amputheater and sit beneath the stars and the moon. I watch the moon as if it might give me some sign.

Stupid.

Horseman continues with his teapot story, and Kitty Boo Boo laughs. I lift off from the roof for no reason, with nowhere to go, only to be closer to the moon. But as I rise I see something in the distance. A shifty black figure moving north across the fields beyond the city, almost invisible except for a luminous white beard.

I take off and follow him. He is old and I overtake him quickly.

"You are stealing away," I tell him. It is Whitebeard who once shared this phrase with me, to *steal away.* To leave without saying goodbye. "Why?"

"Because it's time," he says.

"You think I'll try to stop you. But I won't."

He waits, fluttering in the night wind.

"I won't stop you because it's pointless. All of it."

"Son," he says, his voice gentle, awful.

"Go!" I roar.

I turn from him and flee. Flying blindly, not caring where I go. Wanting nothing to do with any of them, the whole stupid lot of them. Wanting to be alone. Without thinking about it, I fly to the barn where Whitebeard and I often talked.

I alight on the roof and try to clear my head. Far off I can hear a sound. What had Whitebeard called it? Bleating. A bleating sound. Like something pitiable crying out at the whole of the world.

After a time I notice that the night doesn't seem as dark, though the barn is abandoned and though it is still many hours until dawn. I drop down to the ground to investigate, and see that the inside of the barn is glowing behind the doors. So I slip inside.

I cry out when I see what's there. What's there is—everything. Objects of all kinds, stacked on bales of hay and tucked into every space and every corner of the barn. It's like nothing I've ever seen, too much to inventory, all of it shimmering with the ghostlight of memory. Here are tricycles and soccer trophies, a faded blue baby blanket, a pocket watch cracked and rusted, a child's guitar, candlesticks and jump ropes and bowling balls, cowboy boots and high-heeled shoes and roller skates, a sailboat, a model of all the planets moving around the sun, a stuffed tiger with friendly eyes and a bandaged nose, an accordion and a record player, two suits of armor, three swords, and books, dozens of books, no, hundreds of books, heaped in piles that stretch in winding columns from the barn floor to the ceiling. And many, many other things I can't name, all of it sparkling and humming before me.

Whitebeard's treasures.

I'm too stunned to move. And afraid that moving will cause the whole thing to—to disappear, somehow. Instead the trophies and candlesticks and pocket watches and everything else begins to glow even brighter than before, as if electrified, until the inside of the barn is as bright as the moon itself, and then brighter still, so bright that I have to turn away. Soon enough the light begins to fade. I look again at Whitebeard's treasures and see that they're growing dark quickly. Once the color fades, each object breaks apart like so many ashes, falling like gray-black snow on the floor of the barn.

It only takes a few minutes. Then everything is gone. Just—gone.

"Whitebeard!" I cry.

The quiet surrounds me. Maybe it's been quiet this whole time. But it overwhelms me now.

In the shadows of the barn floor something moves. Coalescing from the ashes, it twists and billows, struggling to find a shape. At last it settles into something that looks, maybe, like a tiger. A thin plume of pearly white smoke curls around the back, like a tail. The thing on the barn floor makes a sound then, a whispery wail. A birth wail. It lifts and turns its head, finding me. Unsteady and unsure. Looking to me as if I will somehow have the answers. Any answers.

"Come with me," I say at last. "There is much to learn."

It's cloudy as the night falls. Kitty Boo Boo and I come to rest on a high ridge above the river that divides the city before continuing on into the westward dark. From here we can see the great sweep of the city below us, the streets aglow in the light of a thousand lamp posts. Automobiles inch along the bridge in both directions. The days are growing warmer and the people are moving about with purpose and life.

I scan the skyline until I find, east along the river, the low roof of the factory. It's too far to make out the others clearly, but I know they're there. Worm, Horseman, Rook. And Pearl.

The clouds break and the moon comes into view. In its fullness the gloom lifts, and the city is awash in silver.

She is right, I think. Against all reason, she is right. There is love. Stupid love, hellish love, pointless love.

Beside me, Kitty Boo Boo floats and hums and purrs.

As if she knows anything.

Well. Maybe she does.

So I ask her: "What will we do now?"

She lifts off the ridge, and rises against the moonlit sky. "We watch over them," she calls down to me, "for as long as we can."

I watch her rise. And after a while I follow her.

Acknowledgments

Every book that makes it to print gets a lot of help along the way, and that seems especially true of a book of short stories, which takes shape little by little over the years. Endless thanks to the help, the generosity, and the wisdom of the many people who helped it along in different ways.

To Bret Lott, Dave Jauss, Brian Leung, Abby Frucht and Doug Glover, Clint McCown and Martha Southgate, and all the folks at Vermont College of Fine Arts, for the enthusiasm and the deep, deep knowledge of craft they brought to the writing program; to the editors (and their amazing teams) who've worked on these stories with me over the years, including Katie Berta at *The Iowa Review*, Bek Primrose at *Booth*, Jodee Stanley at *Ninth Letter*, Stephanie G'Schwind at *Colorado Review*, Katy Turner at *Bennington Review*, Janelle Drumwright at *Carve*, Patrick Wilcox and Brad Aaron Modlin at *Quarter After Eight*, Amy Ralston Seife at *The Westchester Review*, and Chase Dearinger at *Arcadia*; to Dewaine Farria, Suzanne Barefoot, Erica Kent, Julian Delfino, and Rhonda Zimlich, for the shared stories, the insights, and the friendship; and to Greg Wolfe and Emily Kwilinski, for their care, their sharp eyes, and their thoughtful suggestions in bringing the book to life.

And finally my family: to Dustin, Brianna, Ethan, and Emma, adults themselves now, for putting up with my sense of humor and keeping me connected to childhood, and not minding when I occasionally lift parts of theirs for a story; and as always and ever, to Abbe, for being my first and best reader, and for coming along with me for the ride. You make every story better.

This book was set in Minion Pro, a typeface created by the renowned designer, Robert Slimbach, and inspired by late-Renaissance typefaces in the humanist style.

This book was designed by Shannon Carter, Ian Creeger, and Gregory Wolfe. It was published in hardcover, paperback, and electronic formats by Slant Books, Seattle, Washington.

Cover: francescoch via Getty Images.

www.ingramcontent.com/pod-product-compliance
Lightning Source LLC
LaVergne TN
LVHW051002080826
845145LV00009B/2414

* 9 7 8 1 6 3 9 8 2 2 2 0 1 *